CRUSADE
OF DORN

ADELARD BASHED OUTWARDS with his storm shield, to give his hammer room to swing. Four of the mutant things were caught by his swipe and sent sprawling into their comrades. His hammerhead boomed with released thunder as he pulverised the chest of the first to rise, plastering his surcoat and armour with blood. The others scuttled away, tangling with their fellows, all of them growling and snapping like dogs. Most had no true power of speech.

'Slay them! Kill them! Cleanse the chapel!' shouted Adelard. 'No pity. No remorse. No fear!'

CALGAR'S SIEGE
An Ultramarines novel by Paul Kearney

BLADES OF DAMOCLES
An Ultramarines novel by Phil Kelly

ANGRON'S MONOLITH
A 'Third War for Armageddon' Relictors novella
by Steve Lyons

THE ETERNAL CRUSADER
A 'Third War for Armageddon' Black Templars novella
by Guy Haley

DANTE'S CANYON
A 'Third War for Armageddon' White Scars novella
by Josh Reynolds

WAR OF THE FANG
A Space Wolves collection by Chris Wraight

THE PLAGUES OF ORATH
An Ultramarines novel by Cavan Scott,
Steve Lyons and Graeme Lyon

DAMNOS
An Ultramarines novel by Nick Kyme

CATECHISM OF HATE
An Ultramarines novella by Gav Thorpe

THE WORLD ENGINE
An Astral Knights novel by Ben Counter

THE SIEGE OF CASTELLAX
An Iron Warriors novel by C L Werner

PANDORAX
A Dark Angels and Grey Knights novel by C Z Dunn

THE PURGING OF KADILLUS
A Dark Angels novel by Gav Thorpe

THE WAR FOR RYNN'S WORLD
A Crimson Fists collection by Steve Parker & Mike Lee

OVERFIEND
A White Scars, Raven Guard and Salamanders novel
by David Annandale

HUNT FOR VOLDORIUS
A White Scars novel by Andy Hoare

MALODRAX
An Imperial Fists novel by Ben Counter

ARMAGEDDON
A Black Templars novel by Aaron Dembski-Bowden

WRATH OF IRON
An Iron Hands novel by Chris Wraight

THE DEATH OF ANTAGONIS
A Black Dragons novel by David Annandale

DEATH OF INTEGRITY
A Blood Drinkers novel by Guy Haley

LEGION OF THE DAMNED
A Legion of the Damned novel by Rob Sanders

FLESH TEARERS
A Flesh Tearers novel by Andy Smillie

THE GILDAR RIFT
A Silver Skulls novel by Sarah Cawkwell

ARCHITECT OF FATE
A linked series of novellas by Sarah Cawkwell, Ben Counter, John French and Darius Hinks

VEIL OF DARKNESS
An Ultramarines audio drama by Nick Kyme

MASTER OF THE HUNT
A White Scars audio drama by Josh Reynolds

TRIALS OF AZRAEL
A Dark Angels audio drama by C Z Dunn

THE ASCENSION OF BALTHASAR
A Dark Angels audio drama by C Z Dunn

Visit blacklibrary.com for the full range of Space Marine Battles novels, novellas, audio dramas and Quick Reads, as well as many other Black Library exclusives

CRUSADERS OF DORN

GUY HALEY

BLACK LIBRARY

A BLACK LIBRARY PUBLICATION

Circle of Honour first published in
Honour of the Space Marines in 2014.
The Black Pilgrims first published digitally in 2014.
Helbrecht: The Crusader first published digitally in 2013.
The Uncanny Crusade first published in this book in 2016.
The Glorious Tomb first published as an audio drama in 2014.
Only Blood first published digitally in 2014.
Season of Shadows first published digitally in 2014.
This edition published in Great Britain in 2016 by
Black Library,
Games Workshop Ltd.,
Willow Road,
Nottingham, NG7 2WS, UK.

10 9 8 7 6 5 4 3 2 1

Produced by Games Workshop in Nottingham.
Cover illustration by Dimitry Burmak

Crusaders of Dorn © Copyright Games Workshop Limited 2016. Crusaders of Dorn, Space Marine Battles, GW, Games Workshop, Black Library, The Horus Heresy, The Horus Heresy Eye logo, Space Marine, 40K, Warhammer, Warhammer 40,000, the 'Aquila' Double-headed Eagle logo, and all associated logos, illustrations, images, names, creatures, races, vehicles, locations, weapons, characters, and the distinctive likenesses thereof, are either ® or TM, and/or © Games Workshop Limited, variably registered around the world.
All Rights Reserved.

A CIP record for this book is available from the British Library.

UK ISBN 13: 978 1 78496 265 4
US ISBN 13: 978 1 78496 266 1

No part of this publication may be reproduced, stored in a retrieval system, or transmitted in any form or by any means, electronic, mechanical, photocopying, recording or otherwise, without the prior permission of the publishers.

This is a work of fiction. All the characters and events portrayed in this book are fictional, and any resemblance to real people or incidents is purely coincidental.

See Black Library on the internet at
blacklibrary.com

Find out more about Games Workshop
and the world of Warhammer 40,000 at
games-workshop.com

Printed and bound by CPI Group (UK) Ltd, Croydon, CR0 4YY

It is the 41st millennium. For more than a hundred centuries the Emperor has sat immobile on the Golden Throne of Earth. He is the master of mankind by the will of the gods, and master of a million worlds by the might of his inexhaustible armies. He is a rotting carcass writhing invisibly with power from the Dark Age of Technology. He is the Carrion Lord of the Imperium for whom a thousand souls are sacrificed every day, so that he may never truly die.

Yet even in his deathless state, the Emperor continues his eternal vigilance. Mighty battlefleets cross the daemon-infested miasma of the warp, the only route between distant stars, their way lit by the Astronomican, the psychic manifestation of the Emperor's will. Vast armies give battle in His name on uncounted worlds. Greatest amongst his soldiers are the Adeptus Astartes, the Space Marines, bioengineered super-warriors. Their comrades in arms are legion: the Astra Militarum and countless planetary defence forces, the ever-vigilant Inquisition and the tech-priests of the Adeptus Mechanicus to name only a few. But for all their multitudes, they are barely enough to hold off the ever-present threat from aliens, heretics, mutants – and worse.

To be a man in such times is to be one amongst untold billions. It is to live in the cruellest and most bloody regime imaginable. These are the tales of those times. Forget the power of technology and science, for so much has been forgotten, never to be re-learned. Forget the promise of progress and understanding, for in the grim dark future there is only war. There is no peace amongst the stars, only an eternity of carnage and slaughter, and the laughter of thirsting gods.

CONTENTS

Circle of Honour	11
The Black Pilgrims	37
Helbrecht: The Crusader	59
The Uncanny Crusade	67
The Glorious Tomb	117
Only Blood	139
Season of Shadows	171

CIRCLE OF HONOUR

The settlement was a foreign object encysted in the forest, crowded by gigantic magenta gynosperms. The sky was a ragged hole two hundred and fifty metres above, heavy with the storm. Through foliage dying from exposure to the wind, the many storeys of the layered ecosystem could be glimpsed. Amid this profusion of xenos life, the homes of men were drab things of plascrete, entirely alien to their setting. This was Bornvel, a backwater outpost of the Imperium. A place of heresy.

Initiate Brusc of the Xereus Crusade stopped his finger on the trigger of his boltgun. The clarity of the moment lent the slight friction of his gauntlet against the trigger as an intolerable weight. He was intimately aware of the grains of dust from the white rain grinding between the metal surfaces. The tendons of his finger were tensed, the ending of an existence a fraction of a millimetre away. Such a small distance between life and oblivion.

'Please,' said the woman kneeling in the mud, her arms protectively around her children. 'Please.'

Pale rain pounded on Brusc's armour, running from its every curve in gritty rivulets. The rain plastered his hair to his scalp and ran into his eyes. It puddled in the hollow at the top of his cuirass, spilling from there in a fidgeting runnel. His tabard was heavy with the rain's silt load, the insignia whitened as if soaked in plaster. A finger of cold wormed its way downward across his chest, the sticky feeling of fresh foam sealant creeping behind it. There was a tiny breach in the heavy plastek of his neckseal. A small wound inflicted on his wargear when his helmet had taken a hit had forced him to discard it.

All the universe telescoped inward. This world, this rebellion, his life, her life, all reduced to one fragment of time – a moment that hinged upon the mechanisms of his weapon, and the will that would set it into action.

Thick smoke rose from the settlement. They had hit the church of the Returning Emperor at the centre first. Other buildings had been targeted and destroyed. They burned only briefly. The downpour put out the blazes, dousing the fury of the Space Marines and sending it out as black fumes to be lost in the towering forest.

The woman and children wore the plain robes of the cult. Only she looked up at the Space Marine – her offspring, a boy of around sixteen standard Terran years and a girl of about six, were bent double, prostrate in the mud. Hands over their faces, they appeared to be praying. Perhaps they were.

His hesitation encouraged the woman. She licked her lips free of the silty rain. 'We did not know we had done wrong, please. We repent! All we wish to do is follow the Emperor. If we honour him incorrectly, teach us,' she pleaded. 'You are an honoured Angel of Death! Have mercy, teach us. Please, please,' she clutched at her motionless children. The boy moaned.

Brusc kept his unwavering aim on the woman. His mind dispassionately ran through what would happen to her should he perform his duty. The firing pin in his gun would detonate the initial propellant charge of the bolt in the chamber. This low-yield explosive would push the round from the barrel at sub-sonic speeds. Once free of the gun, the main propellant load would ignite, accelerating the bolt – in essence a miniature missile – twice the speed of sound over a space of half a metre. The momentum alone would blast the woman apart. After impact, the tiny machine-spirit of the munition would trigger the main charge upon the detection of a preset mass. That might be in her body – should enough of it survive the initial hit – or, if not, the ground. Either way, the woman would be split open, her innards spread between one point six and two metres around her. She would cease to resemble a human being.

The shrapnel would probably kill her children instantly – he calculated sixty-three per cent likelihood for the boy, and seventy-four per cent for the girl. If not, they would die shortly after from their wounds. These probabilities were not good enough. Despite the preciousness of his ammunition, he would also spare a round for both of them, heretics though they were. He would not let them suffer. He was not a monster.

A flight of Land Speeders streaked overhead, grav-plates buzzing. Distant heavy bolter fire sounded from the edge of the town as they banked around. The lesser barks of bolt pistols blurted through the rain. Somewhere, someone was screaming.

Rain poured down his arm, running along the oath chain binding his bolter to his wrist. Drops pattered hurriedly from the links into the milky slur of the street, as if eager to be at one with it.

With one squeeze, he would turn that mud red. It was his duty. It was his oath.

And yet he did not fire.

THE HUMAN PRIOR of *Majesty*'s monasterium bade Brusc halt before the door of the sanctum. He raised his staff, and intoned the ritual request.

'At this date of the year four hundred and twenty-six, millennium forty-one, Terran checksum one, in the tenth millennium of the most holy and beneficent Emperor's reign over the scattered scions of mankind at this time of the third hour of the second watch of the eighty-ninth day of the Madrigal Crusade and upon this, the most holy vessel strike cruiser *Majesty*, blessed be its name and purpose, Brother-Initiate Brusc of the Black Templars Chapter, rightful and most noble heirs to the Primarch Rogal Dorn, may his name ever be sacred, and his most holy champion Sigismund, makes a presentation for his inclusion to the most honourable Brotherhood of the Sword. He would take upon himself its responsibilities and its honours, its oaths and its vows.'

The prior rapped five times upon the doors to the Sanctum of the Majesty. It was a broad entrance, peaked at the apex of the arch, wherefrom glowered the judging face of some long dead ecclesiarch. Brusc had been through that door thousands of times, but today it had a doomy significance that made it novel and disquieting. The preacher was careful not to strike the bold red templar's cross emblazoning the doors, though his staff made no mark upon the black-and-white checked plasteel that surrounded it. 'How does the temple answer?'

From speakers carried by cyber-cherubs fluttering overhead, a deep voice replied, 'Your entreaty is heard, Prior Godwine. Brother Brusc is expected. His presentation is accepted.'

Locks disengaged loudly and the doors parted. Air hissed with slight pressure difference as the seal was breached. Warmer air – redolent of incense, blood and sweat – blew from within.

Prior Godwine bowed, the lengths of the sacred maniple wrapped about his left arm brushed the floor.

'As you command, so I obey, Lord Chaplain Hrollo. Praise be.' The abbot stood and sketched the Templar's cross in the air before his face before turning to Brusc. The Space Marine bowed low and the prior dipped his forefinger and index finger into a silver vessel hanging at his waist. With sanctified rose oil, he drew the Templar's cross upon the crown of Brusc's head.

'You have the blessing of the Emperor, Lord Brusc,' said the prior. 'You may proceed. Praise be.'

Brusc rose, the servos of his armour whining on the edge of hearing. He towered over the human priest. The marks of failed second stage implantation marred the man's skin. It was a wonder he still lived.

'Good luck,' said the prior.

Brusc nodded once. Ordinarily he might have a quip for the man; he was ever being reprimanded for his less than serious nature.

Not today.

He entered the Sanctum as solemn as a High Lord.

NEOPHYTE BRUSC GHOSTED over the moors under a mercilessly open sky, his light scout armour flickering with the false-image camouflage of cameleoline. Heather-like plants stretched off in every direction, heavy with small, tight, blue flowers. Their twigs were slight but tough, closely packed and springy to walk upon. Brusc skimmed his feet carefully through them to avoid breaking the stems. He peered through the heather, avoiding the coarse sand or soft peat that would easily take a footprint. This manner of walking slowed the squad, but the xenos were fine trackers. Whatever the Black Templars could do to obscure their trail, they did.

The four neophytes and their initiate leader did not speak but moved cautiously, eyes watching for the xenos' avian spies when not searching the ground.

Neophyte Parsival laid a hand on Brusc's shoulder. He pointed toward the sun. Hiding in its glare was a deltoid shape.

'You do it, brother. You are the better shot.'

Brusc lowered his visor over his eyes and raised his sniper rifle. The goggles adjusted and compensated for the sunlight, revealing a large, four-winged bird. Brusc zeroed in, and stroked the trigger. The gun's report was a gentle snap, generated by a needle-thin laser beam superheating the air.

The creature's wings folded and it plummeted into the heather. Blue flowers jerked and the avian was gone.

'Good shot,' said Parsival quietly.

'Well,' breathed Brusc. 'I think we can safely say they know we are coming.'

'That they will, neophyte,' said Brother-Initiate Amund, their mentor on this mission. 'Speed will serve us better now than stealth.'

The Templars covered the remaining three kilometres to the edge of the valley swiftly. They fell on their bellies ten metres from the brow of the hill and crawled to the brink.

Many unexpected valleys broke the moorland, steep-sided and deep. They were almost ravines, walled with crags of grey rock that sparkled with veins of quartz. Thin streams knifed along the bottoms, brown and swift. Trees gathered thinly round the boggy land that lined the streams, thickening into forest as the valleys deepened. This valley was no different.

Despite their earlier observation by the aliens' pet, the Black Templars had arrived unannounced. Spindly legged xenos went about their mysterious business. Their camp was split into three collections of tents, clustered on those rare patches of ground both flat and dry. Like their pets, the aliens were hexapods. They utilised all six limbs to propel themselves, rearing up their front third when they needed to bring their foremost paws – somewhat akin to hands – off the earth and into employment. Their throats sported crimson wattles, their skin was elsewhere smooth and pink where it was not banded brown with natural, keratinous armour plates.

'Filth,' spat Parsival. 'I've not seen such degenerates before.'

'Oh,' said Brusc mildly. 'And your career in our order is already long and glorious.'

Parsival elbowed Brusc hard below the pauldron, where his arm was unarmoured. Once there were such amity blows, but rivalry had made them sharper. The longer they had been members of the Chapter, and the more their fellow recruits dwindled in number, the more they had grown apart in temperament.

'Silence,' whispered Amund. 'Concentrate on your task, or my report to your knights will not be favourable.' The initiate scanned the valley. 'Neophyte Lothic,' he asked. 'Give the squad a good course of action.'

'Assassinate their leadership and retreat,' Lothic replied instantly. 'We are ordered here on a disruption strike, and are well placed to execute our orders and be away before the xenos can respond.'

'Those are indeed our orders,' said Amund. 'You listened. Praise be.'

Parsival disagreed. 'We should deploy two of us there.' He pointed at a crag whose top extended above the lip of the valley. 'One there and one there,' he said, indicating two other locations. 'I'd say work our way around the head of the valley, attack from two sides, but they have many of their eyes here.' A long perch was in the middle of the camp. The aliens' metre-high birds were tethered to it, hoods over their eyes. 'We risk discovery the longer we take.'

'If speed is of the essence, why then not attack from one place?' asked Amund.

'We will sow confusion amongst them. They are primitive with little knowledge of firearms. They will locate us slowly if we are dispersed. Should one group attack, then the other pair may offer fire support. We can then withdraw once their leaders are dead. It is a balance. Expediency versus perfection.'

Amund pursed his lips and nodded. 'A not entirely foolish strategy, Neophyte Parsival. And what will my role be in this?'

Brusc spoke before Parsival could respond. 'You role, brother, is to watch over Parsival, and ensure he does not slip and fall in his excitement.'

Amund scowled. 'Your levity is rarely welcome, Neophyte Brusc. You shall be disciplined for this when we returned.'

Brusc's crooked smile vanished from his face.

'Now, perhaps you have something better to add? If not–'

'Actually, brother-initiate, I do,' Brusc interrupted. Amund motioned for him to continue. 'Parsival's split fire pattern is sound, although I would advise the placing of the second group further along the valley lip. The xenos will see us quickly enough, if they get their hawks into the air. Moving a little further out won't take much longer. I agree with Parsival that the further apart we are the better.'

'So you suggest caution?'

Brusc's smile returned. 'No, I advise that we finish every last one of them!'

'Those are not our orders,' said Amund reasonably. There was invitation to disagree in his voice. 'Thirty-six of them and five of us. Are these good odds?'

'Thirty-six alien filth and five Black Templars, brother. We are a forward group acting partly under our own initiative. This escalation of our goals is fitting, given the circumstances, and achievable.'

Amund nodded. 'See here, our sharp-tongued warrior might make a fool of himself, but he has the making of a true crusader. If presented with an opportunity to further the Emperor's plan, we should take it. Recklessness is a fool's trait, and brings the fool's reward of death. But ours is not a timid order. Where it is possible to attack, to advance, without undue risk, then it is our duty to do so. Those are our ways. Brusc reminds us of them. Praise be.'

'Praise be,' responded the others, some more enthusiastically than others.

In five minutes the neophytes had worked their way into position. They waited, tense with expectation. Often in their impatience they looked from their gunsights to the place where their leader was hidden, indistinguishable from the heather in his cameleoline. Long minutes, then hours, saw the yellow sun track painfully through the sky. Small biting insects vexed them.

When the sun westered, shining from behind the Black Templars, Amund finally gave the order to open fire.

The aliens were preparing their evening meal and were taken unawares. The first shot belonged to Parsival. The alien's head jerked back and it half turned, half reared as its left-hand leg set folded underneath it. With a sinuous motion, it toppled onto the short turf. The sound of the sniper rifle was a clack as quiet as a kicked pebble, and the fiend's death went unnoticed for vital seconds. Annoyed Parsival had beaten him, Brusc dropped two more in quick succession. 'He should have gone for the falconer,' he said, and cursed the lack of a clear line of sight to this most prominent target from his own position. By the time the second of his marks had died, the camp had erupted.

The xenos ran about, greatly agitated. They snatched up weapons – slender, stone-tipped spears and atlatls to cast them, along with those few guns of low technology treasonously supplied them by the Hamadad Collective. Their falconer whipped the hoods and leashes from his charges and had several of the large avians into the air before his brains were finally blasted out. The birds flew unerringly toward the neophyte's position. The aliens followed the line of their falcon's flight, pointing and hooting to the hilltop. Running on five limbs, the sixth holding their weapons free of the ground, the aliens galloped up the hill towards the Space Marines quicker than horses

Brusc drew a bead on one heading right for him, and a dark shape blurred past his scope and his shot went wild. He rolled over to see the avian arresting its ascent to swoop down at him. Four wings buffeted the Scout, talons raking his face. He held his rifle crosswise over his chest as the bird scrabbled for his fingers with its claws. Brusc slammed it with his gun butt. The bird let out a piercing shriek and flapped away erratically, its wing injured. But the creature had bought valuable time for its masters. The xenos Brusc would surely have killed crested the ridge. A sweet stink came with it. Brusc discarded his sniper rifle and launched himself backwards, pulling his bolt pistol free. The things were as quick in their reactions as they were on their feet, and his opponent knocked his gun out of his hand with a slash of its spear. Brusc hurled himself at the alien. They grappled, Brusc's head pressed horrifically close to its broad face. They locked eyes, his clear brown to its widely set pupil-less black orbs. Hatred blazed equally from both.

The aliens were devilishly strong, and Brusc found himself grasped tight by its foremost two sets of limbs while it reared to its full height on its back legs. He shoved back, and they fell down the steep slope together. The creature rolled itself into a tight ball, its hooves and hands ripping at the Space Marine trapped inside the circuit of its body. They bounced rapidly to the valley floor, landing with a splash in the stream. Brusc wrenched out his combat knife and buried it to the hilt in between the thing's armour segments. It convulsed once, squeezing him painfully, then flopped open. Brusc pushed the corpse aside.

A couple of the aliens had made the valley brink, where they duelled with Brusc's brothers, and many more littered the slopes. He watched one jerk backwards, a huge crater in its side leaking yellow fluid, felled by Amund's bolt pistol.

One came at him, feet splashing in the marsh. Brusc reached for his own pistol, but found an empty holster. His knife remained in the dead xenos. He searched the ground for a weapon as the alien came at him, brandishing a stone axe as big as a man's torso.

The mud dragged at Brusc's boots as he reached for the dead alien's spear. Both projectile and atlatl had fallen into the bog, but still he snatched the spear up. It was proportionate to the alien's size, too big for a human. Nevertheless Brusc used it expertly, fitting the spear to the caster and hurling it with deadly force right into the alien's eye.

The creature tumbled over, skidding to a stop in front of Brusc.

The noise of battle was dying. Of the three dozen aliens, only ten remained, and half of these were running. Shots rang out uselessly from the creatures as they fell back. They were unused to such weapons, and they were of poor quality. Two more died from sniper shots before the xenos made it around a kink of the valley and to safety.

Victory was shouted from the valley sides, but Brusc was silent. His attention was fixed upon an amulet hanging from his second kill's neck: a piece of exquisitely carved amber. The work seemed too fine to have been made by such brutish hands. He bent forward to pick it up, his hatred for the creatures replaced by curiosity.

'Hold there, brother,' said Amund, approaching from behind. He squelched into the bog. 'We do not take trophies from the likes of these. This is xenos work, unclean. Unfit to adorn a member of the Adeptus Astartes. Let the serf recorders take what they will for the Museum of Eradication. Brothers and neophytes shall not touch the work of the alien – that is the rule of our order.'

Brusc looked at his leader. He withdrew his hand.

'A good tactical choice, neophyte Brusc,' said Amund approvingly. 'This world is closer to enjoying the holy tread of human feet thanks to you. Soon these things will be extinct.' He gestured around the battlesite. 'Now aid your brothers in gathering this filth up. Burn them all.'

BEFORE HE WAS permitted into the chapel, Brusc was stripped of his armour. He was taken into a plain antechamber he had never set eyes on before. Monks from the Monasterium deep in the bowels of *Majesty* waited for him within. They swarmed him, their faces pictures of furious devotion, and chanted the orisons of hatred as they tore at his oath papers, their fingernails scrabbling on his armour.

The tabard he had so carefully prepared for the ritual was wrenched from him, the fine embroidery of his name, crusades, worlds he had scoured and foes he had killed were torn to shreds. 'This is the mark of an initiate. You aspire to a higher order,' said the human preacher who ripped it free. Brusc kept his eyes ahead, emotionless.

Another took a sharp flint and gouged a scratch across the Templar's cross adorning his left shoulder pad. 'Black for the brothers, red for the Inner Circle!' The monk slit his palm open and smeared his blood over the cross.

From the other, his parchments of supplication were ripped.

'Kneel!' the lead preacher commanded. 'In the name of the Emperor, kneel!'

Brusc did so. Armoury servitors clumped out of alcoves, the fine keys and screwdrivers upon their multiple arms whirring. The servitors disengaged his armour's bolts, unclasped the points, and the monks roughly took his battleplate from him. Then they scourged his bare flesh with whips, each serf naming a failing of Brusc's before he struck. He bore the stings of their weak blows without complaint or reaction.

When they panted from their exertions, they left. Shortly after, Brother Chaplain Hrollo entered the room.

'Are you ready?' he asked gruffly. He wore his full war regalia: ornate power armour bedecked with skull and bones, some representations cast in plasteel or carved into the ceramite, the others relics of his honoured predecessors bolted to the larger plates. The cant of the Templars was chased into the burnished black surface in red gold. Brusc had never seen Hrollo's face, only and always the helmet cast in the shape of a skull.

Brusc stared ahead still.

'Yes, Brother-Chaplain.'

'Then I will begin,' Hrollo said, laying a heavy hand upon Brusc's head. 'In omnibus operibus tuis in conspectu Imperatoris,' intoned the Chaplain in richly rolling High Gothic.

'In the sight of the Emperor are all my deeds,' responded Brusc, his voice little more than a whisper.

'Imperatoris sunt verba audiente toto,' continued the Chaplain.

'In the hearing of the Emperor are all my words,' said Brusc.

'In cogitatione tua pietas Imperatoris,' said the Chaplain.

'My devotion is in the thoughts of the Emperor.'

'Tu quoque filius eius vindicem. Tu quoque filius eius militem.'

'I am his champion, I am his soldier.'

'Dignus es fides?'

'I am worthy of his trust,' said Brusc.

'Et vos accipere stabit?' asked Hrollo.

'I accept the challenge gladly.'

'Ita fiat. So be it. Praise be,' the Chaplain concluded. 'Brother Brusc, initiate of the Black Templars Chapter, son of Rogal Dorn, you may enter the Circle of Honour. Praise be to His name, and to His holy mission.'

'Leave him!' said Mekal. He tugged at Garsanhuk's sleeve. 'He has failed the test.'

Garsanhuk looked helplessly at his friend, Ketekehan. He had expected that not all of them would survive the trial, that they would die in the Forbidden Lands of Fergax. Seeing it was another matter entirely. Ketekehan was unconscious, his leg swallowed by a pit in the sparse grass and impaled upon a gleaming spike of rustless metal.

'They left it here, the star warriors. He did not see it. It is a part of the trial. He is not worthy!'

'If we leave him, he will die,' said Garsanhuk. Already Ketekehan's skin had gone a ghostly white, and Garsanhuk's hands were red with his blood. 'His bleeding will not stop.'

'He will die anyway even if we save him!' said Mekal. 'The star warrior said there was only death or success. No other way. He knew this as well as you or I do.'

Garsanhuk got to his feet reluctantly. The pit in the sandy soil was shallow and filling with blood.

'Come on now,' said Mekal, encouragingly. 'We are aiding each other. This is a rare thing. Do you think Jukal or Velatahan will help each other?'

Garsanhuk shook his head slowly.

'See! I feel sorry for Ketekehan. He is my friend also. But we are different, hey? We are as good as brothers. That's why we'll win. We're going, you and I. We're going to join the war in the stars! Brothers forever?' Mekal held out his hand.

Garsanhuk smiled wanly and grasped Mekal's forearm. 'Brothers forever.'

'Come on! It's getting late. If you feel sorry for him, offer him mercy.' He patted his knife.

Garsanhuk looked from Mekal to Ketekehan. 'I can't.'

'How many throats have you cut?'

Garsanhuk shrugged. 'Ten?'

'Then why not eleven?'

'Because this is Ketekehan, not some driftspinner from the woods!'

Mekal shook his head. 'Gar, Gar, Gar! Always ready with some joke or other, but underneath the bluster you're soft. This is a *kindness*. The krossovore will get him. Do you want him to be eaten alive, because I don't. If you won't, I'll do it.'

Mekal pulled out his own knife, a fine weapon forged

by his father, its furniture carved from the tooth of one of ferocious predators of Fergax. He slit Ketekehan's throat adroitly. The other boy did not wake. The pulse of blood from his neck was sluggish.

'Nearly dead already anyway,' said Mekal. He stabbed his knife into the ground to clean it before he sheathed it. 'But it is better to be sure.' He set off at a jog. 'If we hurry, we'll make the third marker by nightfall!' he called back.

With a backwards glance for their dead friend, Karsanhuk set out after Mekal.

A PLAIN RING of sand fifteen metres across in a room of unadorned metal – that was one manifestation of the Circle of Honour. A single strong lumen globe shone directly above it, lighting the sand as bright as any desert, but leaving its margins in shadow. There in darkness stood hooded Black Templars. This was the other manifestation of the Circle of Honour – the Sword Brotherhood to which Brusc aspired. Here were the Crusade's mightiest warriors and officers and they waited in judgement.

They parted ranks to allow Brusc into the ring. His and Hrollo's footsteps spoiled the perfect surface. The armoured Hrollo sank deep into the sand. Brusc less so, naked but for a loincloth.

Hrollo held up Brusc's hand. 'Here is an aspirant to the inner circle of our Chapter. Is he worthy of the challenge?'

'Aye,' said one.

'He is.'

'Yes,' said another.

One after another the Sword Brethren gave their consent. None bar the crusade's three Chaplains wore armour. Their faces were hidden by black hoods. Half-blinded by the harsh spotlight, Brusc struggled to pick out the individual heraldries embroidered upon the tabards below their red Sword Brothers' crosses. He knew them all, of course. Somewhere among them would be Brother Castellan Adelard, his one-time mentor, and the crusade's second-in-command. Only then did Brusc notice that there were twenty-three brothers there, not the twenty-two he expected.

'It is decided. He is worthy,' said Hrollo, when the last brother had spoken. A Chapter-serf, one who had voluntarily undergone the removal of his eyes and ears so that he might serve this most august body without betraying it, came into the ring. He knelt and held up a longsword in a rich scabbard. For a pommel, it had a Templar's cross cast in brass and was sized for the giants of the Space Marines, but otherwise it could have been a knight's weapon of ancient Terra.

'This is the Sword of Challenge, hallowed by the blood of failed aspirants to our order. You will only ever hold its like within this circle. Be honoured. Now draw it, and test your mettle,' commanded Hrollo.

Brusc did so. He tested the weapon's heft and balance, and sighted down the plain steel edge. It was a very fine blade. He pressed the crossguard to his lips and kissed it, muttering a quick prayer to the Emperor. He took up a guard stance, blade gripped in both hands up by his right shoulder.

'Send in his opponent!' called Hrollo. He held up his crozius arcanum and let it fall, stepping to the side of the ring. 'To first blood! Praise be!'

The twenty-third brother stepped forward, and pulled down his hood.

'We meet again, brother.'

'Parsival?' asked Brusc. His guard wavered.

'Surprised to see me, art thou?' Parsival said mockingly. 'The test must be completed to certain forms. Brothers forever, we used to say on Fergax. Who better to test a man than those closest to him?'

A pair of serfs came forward and removed Parsival's robe. Underneath he was dressed as Brusc, naked but for his loincloth.

'They brought me here especially for this trial. I am one of them now, had you not heard? I am ahead of you now as I always was.' Parsival smiled. He had always been colder, more driven than Brusc, even when he had been Mekal. But an arrogance had bloomed in him that Brusc did not like. 'Twenty years it's been since we fought side by side.' Parsival took an axe and a spike-headed flail from the arming serf. 'Shall we see what you have learned?'

With that he launched himself at Brusc. He held the flail back, bringing the axe down hard towards his one-time friend's head. Brusc parried it fluidly and circled back.

'I am the match of you, Sword Brother or not,' said Brusc. He was not as sure as he appeared. Who knew what Parsival had learned himself in the last two decades?

Parsival spun the head of his flail round until it whooshed noisily. 'I have outgrown your skill at arms.'

Parsival swung with the mace, entrapping Brusc's sword with the weapon when he parried. The axe followed. Brusc was ready. Taking a swift backwards pivot he yanked the flail from Parsival's hand, moved aside from the axe blow. Parsival was pulled forward, leaving him at the mercy of a hard strike from the pommel of Brusc's sword.

Parsival fell down, stunned. Blood welled from his

head, though the wound was quickly staunched by the blood-gift of the Emperor.

'You might be right. Perhaps you are the better Black Templar, dear Parsival,' said Brusc looking down at his friend. 'But we both know I have always been the better warrior.'

'The test is decided. Brusc has triumphed, and swiftly,' said Hrollo. 'Praise be!'

'Praise be,' replied the knights of the Inner Circle.

Brusc reached a hand down to Parsival. After a moment's hesitation, he took it. 'Well fought,' said Brusc. Parsival managed a grudging nod of acknowledgement.

'Long have we watched you. By your skill at arms here, you have proved our assessment of your abilities correct. Now, you have one last test to pass,' said Hrollo.

The circle of knights parted and the Chaplain gestured to a slim door they revealed. It was as plain as if it were the portal to a prison cell.

Brusc looked to the faces of the Sword Brothers and war-priests around the challenge circle, but they looked away from him. Only Hrollo's ruby helmet lenses stayed upon his face.

Brusc took a deep breath and tipped his sword forward. The flail rattled down its length and fell to the floor. The door opened at his approach and closed behind him, sealing him into a thick gloom.

The room on the other side was also circular and bare of adornment, but smaller than the first. A larger door faced the small entrance. In front of it stood a Dreadnought, Ironclad class. The hard lines of its armour were picked out by the light of two flambeaux leaning out from the walls on chains. Otherwise, the room was unlit.

The dreadnought was inert. His name was engraved deeply into scrollwork upon the sarcophagus: *Cantus Maxim Gloria*. Honour scrolls and a prayer cloth were affixed all over the machine. The Templar's cross – worked in the red and black of the Sword Brotherhood – repeated over and again upon his joints. The mounts for his carapace weapons gleamed bare, but his arms had been mounted for reasons of balance. On the left it carried a power fist and on the right a hurricane bolter, both lavishly worked with Cantus's deeds and name. The crusade honours that covered its shoulder plating were perforce rendered small, such was Cantus Maxim Gloria's honourable history. They referred not only to the current occupant's accomplishments, but to those of the men who had been entombed within before him, stretching back to the dawn of the Imperium.

Brusc dropped to his knees, his sword point down upon the floor. This was the crusade ancient, and one of the oldest living members of the Black Templars. Once a templar was granted this ultimate respect, he gave up his prior existence. Thus few knew who the warrior was interred within, but all were in awe of his wisdom.

With a rumble, the machine's engines started. With a jerk like a man emerging abruptly from sleep, Cantus came online. The chambers of his hurricane bolter clicked as internal systems checked its status. He rose higher as the hydraulic systems in his limbs pressurised and his fibre bundles contracted. It looked from side to side, then leaned forward over Brusc, power fist whirring.

'You are the reason I have been awoken from my long slumber,' said Cantus.

'I assume so, crusade ancient. The mysteries of initiation are not revealed until they are undertaken.'

'Hrrrn.' Cantus's growl from his vox amplifiers might or might not have conveyed humour. 'I have been told of you, Brother-Initiate Brusc. You are light of tongue, if heavy in honour. It is your doom to be judged by me. Will you hear my verdict?'

'I will, brother ancient.'

'I fear you shall not like it, brother.'

Brusc's blood, still running hotly from his test in the ring, chilled instantly. He looked up at the Dreadnought. The armourglass slit in the sarcophagus glowed an eerie green, like the eyes of a dog in low light. 'What do you mean?'

'Heh, you forget your manners in your shock. You know what I mean!' said the machine. 'You are not worthy to join the Sword Brethren, not yet. Do not despair. You are strong of arm and will. But it is not yet your time.'

'But, why?' said Brusc. He felt no outrage, which surprised him. 'I beat Parsival... Is it my faith? Is it my–'

The Dreadnought shifted its weight, an unconscious movement that recalled Cantus's time as a man. The noise of his foot on the deck as he resettled himself rang loudly.

'It is not your faith. Your faith is strong, Brother-Initiate Brusc. Nor is strength at arms the only qualification for acceptance to the Circle. Remind me of our motto, Black Templar.'

'No pity! No remorse! No fear!' shouted Brusc, the words pouring from him with pride and at full war volume. They boomed in the chamber.

'Yes, yes!' Cantus leaned back slightly. 'These words were not lightly chosen, initiate. Our creed is to pursue the enemies of the Emperor to the ends of the universe, to never cease in spreading the reach of His holy light. You are his instrument. Does a sword have a conscience? No! It is thrust where the warrior who bears it wills it to go. You are a sword in the hand of the Emperor. That is what it means to be a Sword Brother. Not only to be a master of the blade, but to be the blade of the highest, most holy master – the Lord of Mankind – and to act unthinkingly under his guidance. I have reviewed many of your battles, watched the pict captures of your helm. There is yet too much mercy in you. You are not an arbiter, but the deliverer of judgement. Remember that, and your next admission to this room will prove more successful.'

The door behind Cantus Maxim Gloria squealed open.

'Now depart, Brother-Initiate Brusc. Wakefulness is taxing, and my sepulchre calls to me. I have been otherwise impressed by the deeds I have witnessed and if half what the others say of you is accurate, then I am proud to fight beside you.'

Cantus turned, an awkward manoeuvre for so noble a machine. One foot remained in place as the other stumped about in a half circle. He rocked from side to side as he moved. Once he had attained a half rotation, he walked from the room, his giant feet banging thunderously upon the deck. Brusc's face fell.

It took some time before he had gathered himself sufficiently to go back into the Place of Challenge and face the others.

THE WOMAN STARED into Brusc's eyes. As far as he could tell, this sect had done little to deviate from the norm of the Imperial Cult. He had seen far more divergent churches tolerated. Why were they here?

His conscience troubled him. He had taken an oath. There were to be no survivors. The heretics were to be expunged. At least these would have a clean death. Already the Ministorum preachers that dwelt aboard *Majesty* were building great iron fire cages to purify those who had strayed from the true path.

The credo of his order was that of crusade – the liberation of worlds and the expansion of the Emperor's realm. Instead he was upon an Imperial world, about to execute frightened children in their mother's arms. Who was he to deliver their judgement? Let some other dirty their hands. His gun wavered. Gritting his teeth, he brought it back to bear on the woman, before giving up completely.

With an explosive exhalation, he put up his gun. His cheeks burned with shame.

'Get out of here,' he said hoarsely. 'Go on, repent. Be true to the teachings of the one true faith until the end of your days, or as I stand here before you I swear I shall hunt you down and kill you all.'

The woman let out a sound halfway between a sob and a laugh. She pulled herself from the quagmire. With frantic, shaking hands, she pulled her catatonic children up after her.

'Thank you, thank you!' she said.

'I do not want your thanks!' said Brusc. 'Get out of here!'

They staggered into the sheeting rain, slipping in the mud and disappearing out of sight around the side of a monolithic forestry machine.

With the weakness of his mercy leaden in his chest, Brusc returned to the fight.

THE BLACK PILGRIMS

A CATHEDRAL SHIP was an immensity. They had no class, mark or design. Each was unique, a baroque fancy fashioned by the faithful to divine and ineffable plans.

The *Veritas Diras* was seven million tons of sculpted stone carved from a single asteroid. The harsh and unforgiving soul of a pilgrimage fleet, built to bring the radiance of the Emperor the worlds of the Imperium. It reflected a cold, lunar light from its marmoreal splendour, no warmth to its albedo glare.

Missing for three centuries, it was lost no longer.

The *Veritas Diras* had emerged from the warp into the far reaches of Goshan. At that distance from the system's heart, the sun was an orange star not much larger than all the others. A world of ammoniac ice passed behind the *Veritas Diras*, bright as a coin. These were the dead marches. The cathedral ship was a monument in the graveyards of space. The beauty of its parapets and carved buttresses, of its towering statues of saints and heroes and the kilometres-long, double-eagle-headed prow, had become the stark beauty of a flensed skull, final and lifeless. Grand oriels and gallery casements reflected starlight, allowing none within. Blackness swam behind toothed mullions, secrets hidden by a skeletal grin.

This shrine-ship to the undying God-Emperor had become a mausoleum, an architectural death's-head heretically presaging His final end.

A handful of other vessels attended the cathedral, caught in its weak gravity well.

Of the rest of the fleet that had set sail with it – many hundreds strong, and the millions of faithful that they had borne along the Macharian circuit – there was no sign.

'This is an affront to the almighty Emperor,' spoke Brother Godwin. 'It is blasphemy!'

There were five of them. Black Templars, Sword Brothers, the veterans of the Dominar Crusade. They watched the dead ship through their helm displays, viewing feeds routed to them from their assault shuttle's augurs. Dim red lighting bathed them in a sanguinary glow, making their black armour dark as murder and their white helmets and bone-coloured surcoats the scarlet of gore.

'Three hundred years in the warp – I expected more damage,' said Brother Ercus. More analytical than his brothers, he was yet devout through and through. There was no doubt that his heart belonged to the Emperor – nevertheless, he did not allow his piety to overwhelm him. He was a welcome check on the others.

'The light of the Lord of Man would have kept it safe. That is a holy vessel,' said Brother Morholt, the pilot of the assault

shuttle, over the vox. *'Proof, surely, against even the worst the warp can conjure.'*

'I do not think so. The ship's body is pristine, brother,' said Sword Brother Rolan. 'The same cannot be said for its soul. It has no doubt been polluted by the warp, its crew and passengers devoured.'

He shifted in his restraints, hefting the heavy flamer grasped in his fist. He was eager to unleash its cleansing fire.

'The forge reports the Geller fields intact,' Castellan Adelard, their leader, said. 'Thermal signatures indicate both reactors are active.'

'Engines?' enquired Mallas, the last of their group. He was a man of few words.

'Offline,' said Adelard. 'The ship is dead.'

'Not dead, its spirit lives,' Dolus, the Crusade's forgemaster, interjected. He and his Techmarines travelled in a second shuttle alongside the Sword Brethren's. A third trailing the first pair carried more of their battle-brothers, the power-armoured initiates. *'I have a reading on the central cogitator banks. Quiescent, but alive.'*

'You can rouse it?' asked Mallas.

'Of course.' Dolus's voice popped with star-born interference. *'It has slept only a few centuries. All organic components are dead. Servitor-led systems have perished, but the machine-spirits wait patiently for the touch of the faithful.'*

'Life signs?' asked Adelard.

'It is hard to say, my lord. The vessel is carved into solid rock with a high iron content. I will have no definitive answer until we are closer.'

The trio of black-skinned shuttles set their retro burners, slowing them as they drew nearer to the cathedral ship. They passed beneath a lesser vessel.

'Light escort cruiser,' said Adelard. He targeted reticules in his visor, each centring on the armaments projecting from its sides. Each muzzle was fashioned in the form of a gargoyle. The stanchions between gun blocks were cast as angels – hands clasped, eyes looking upwards.

'I see no damage here either,' said Ercus.

A thumbnail screen in Adelard's visor showed Ercus's view. The Sword Brother was rapidly scanning the nearest vessels. 'There is no damage to any of them.'

'Then it is as reported. They were not overtaken by raiders,' said Adelard.

'The mystery deepens,' said Ercus. 'Genestealers, perhaps.'

'Pah! There is no mystery,' said Brother Rolan. 'Warp intrusion. It is as I said. Genestealers could not infest an entire fleet. You are wrong, brother!'

'Care to take a wager?' asked Ercus.

'Let us not make assumptions, best be wary for all eventualities,' said Adelard. 'Even you, Brother Rolan, as old as you are, have not seen all that the galaxy has to offer.'

The others laughed good-naturedly. Rolan made an exasperated noise. A fine fighter he was, perhaps the best of the Crusade's veterans, but he spent more time doing penance than any of them.

The shuttle coasted under the giant, holy vessel. It was as big as a battleship, an ornate sphere as regal as a king's orb, and the long prow and stern extending from its equatorial diameter made it appear transfixed by a sword. The shuttles circled it once, then again. The Sword Brothers watched intently, searching for signs of weapon damage or hull breaches. There were none.

'All entries are sealed. Blast doors shut,' Morholt reported. *'This vessel was placed in lockdown.'*

'Forgemaster Dolus, can you access the ship's systems and open the way within?'

'Regrettably I cannot, castellan. I will need to interface directly with the machine-spirits of the cathedral ship. Once they are roused, remote operations will be child's play. For now, they hide behind their code-walls and will pay no heed to me.'

'Then select us a landing site that will allow quiet entrance,' said Adelard.

'There is window, a lesser chapel, here.'

A wireframe schematic scrolled up the inside of Adelard's visor; Dolus's suggested ingress blinked red. Adelard nodded, impatiently clearing with a thought-command the screeds of information cluttering his view. He was ready for action. They all were.

'Brother Morholt, follow Brother Dolus's recommendation. Bring us in. Enough of this reconnaissance.'

His brothers voxed their glad agreement. 'Always forward,' said Rolan, 'never back. That is the way of the Black Templars.'

'Aye!' shouted the others. 'Onwards for the glory of the Emperor!'

The shuttle travelled vertically relative to the cathedral ship, its heavily decorated skin scant metres away from the Black Templars prow. Grand statues slipped by, expansive canyons of carved stone plunged deep into the hull. The shuttle passed between two buttresses the size of fleet tenders. A tall window was before them.

There was a silent flash and the window sagged inwards, slagged by the assault craft's melta array. Plasteel shutters on the inside of the windows shone with white heat and collapsed. Air blasted from the breach, buffeting the ship. Morholt played the weapons over the window, until he had cut out a gap large enough to allow the craft inside. The rush of air gave out and Morholt piloted them carefully within.

Darkness enveloped them. The shuttle jolted.

'The gravitic plates here are functional,' said Morholt.

The shuttle's lights snapped on and tiny discs of illumination played over silent stone saints – a lesser chapel, yet still mighty. Morholt put the craft down near the chapel's doors, some two hundred metres inside the ship. The other shuttles followed, landing not far from the first. They faced the doors, ready to bring their weapons to bear should the need arise.

The landing ramp of Adelard's vessel opened. With metallic clunks felt and not heard, the mag-harnesses securing their Terminator suits disengaged. 'Sword Brothers, forward,' he said over the vox.

The Terminators filed out, passing from the shuttle's light into the chapel's gloom. The initiates ran out of their own craft, soundless in the vacuum, their swift deployment in a defensive circle registered as tremors upon the Sword Brothers' suit senses. Dolus and his two acolytes came out of their own craft last, servo-harnesses unfurling as they cleared the hatchway.

Adelard investigated the chapel with all the technology his suit possessed. He sent his brothers out from him to widen the net. Their faith lanterns flickered at their waists, representing their undying zeal to bring the light of the Imperium's rule to the darkness. Suit-lamps, far brighter, stabbed out from their hunched carapaces to chase off the night.

'No signs of damage, brother,' they said, one after another.

Adelard approached the side of the chapel. The floor was stone, cracked under the weight of the shuttles. The panels of the walls were of dark bronze inscribed with devotional scriptures. He glanced towards the broken window.

'We shall do penance of thirteen nights for the destruction wrought upon this holy place,' he intoned. 'Unwillingly we destroy that which is sacred to the Emperor. May the light of Terra forgive us for our misdemeanours, though committed as they are during the course of our duties.'

'We ask forgiveness of the Lord of Man,' responded his brothers.

'Forgemaster Dolus, attend to your prayers. We shall see if they will rouse the machine-spirits. Initiate Brusc, ensure that he does so unharried.'

'We are eager to accompany you, my lord,' Brusc protested.

'I approve of your desire to engage, brother, but a defensive perimeter must be maintained. You will remain here. Protect the forge.'

'Yes, castellan,' said Brusc, bowing his head. 'As you wish it.'

THE SWORD BROTHERS lumbered through echoing corridors, their backs swaying. They pushed on past chapel after chapel, thoroughly checking each for the presence of evil. They found none, only the stone faces of saints glaring in their suit-lamp beams. The squad flicked through their numerous sensor arrays without thinking. Infrared overlays gave them nothing but the chill landscapes of forgotten presbyteries, while echolocators sketched funereal monuments in sound. Motion trackers caught only their own progress.

Atmosphere persisted in the inner halls, but it was stale and poisonous. They breathed suit air, ripe with their own scents and the harsh, vinegary stink of carbon scrubbers. Their armoured boots clanged obscenely loudly in the silence, mag-locks clamping hard where gravity gave out.

'Truly,' said Mallas, dolorously, 'this place of devotion has become nought but a tomb.'

They came at last to a set of great plasteel doors, every inch chased in gold depicting scenes from the Emperor's life. The Space Marines halted in front of it, awed by its beauty. They muttered quick prayers and brought their weapons up to their faceplates, longing to kiss the killing edges of their blades and mauls in obeisance to the God of Men.

'Sealed,' said Ercus, who had recovered quicker than the rest. His upper torso rotated, away from the door switches hidden in exquisitely wrought miniature churches of alien wood. 'The mechanisms are dead, their spirits fled.'

He rejoined his brothers. Terminator plate was clumsy and cumbersome, its heavy plating and restrictive range of movement made most wearers ungainly. Yet, somehow, Ercus managed to remain graceful.

Adelard thought out to his suit's cogitator, commanding it to capture every square centimetre of the door. 'The Black Templars will recreate this object, this I swear. I shall do it myself if needs be.'

'A good oath, brother,' said Godwin.

'A necessary one. Now, break it down.'

Godwin advanced slowly in contrast to Ercus. However, he was nigh on unstoppable in battle. 'My hammer is sorrowed by this work,' he said.

'Have Dolus pray to its spirit to placate it,' said Adelard. 'And assure it that you shall smite those who are forcing us to undertake this defilement.'

'Yes, castellan,' said Godwin. With a snap and flare of soapy blue energy, Godwin's thunder hammer came to life.

They left the door broken behind them.

'Forgemaster,' reported Adelard. 'We have gained the tertiary transept. We are making our way to the nave.'

'*Acknowledged*,' Dolus replied, his voice faint.

The nave ran the length of the ship, kilometres long and hundreds of metres high. Interstellar night lurked in the vaulting high overhead. Faces of the devout, carved from the chill rock of the asteroid that made the cathedral ship, appeared suddenly from the gloom before vanishing just as quickly.

Adelard led from the front, as it should be. A Black Templar never held back from the fight. His hammer's disruption field was active and eager. His storm shield hummed on his other arm.

Ercus, Godwin and Mallas followed – Godwin's own hammer spitting with fury, Ercus and Mallas's lightning claws gleaming with a quieter, more sinister light. Rolan went protected in their centre, his heavy flamer ready.

'Keep close watch, brothers. We are exposed here,' said Adelard.

'Something is in the way ahead. Residual organic traces, and metal,' said Ercus, gesturing to an irregular heap furred with dust.

'Cyber-cherubim,' said Adelard. He clumped over to the fragile remains: child's bones tangled with age-dulled iron.

'Someone has heaped these here,' observed Mallas. 'There are seven or eight of them.'

'Eight,' Ercus confirmed. 'This suggests that whatever befell these people, there were survivors. Still convinced it is the denizens of the empyrean, Rolan?'

'We'll see,' said Rolan. 'I'll not tolerate your boasting until we are sure.'

'Genestealers, brother. I am sure of it,' said Ercus, the smile in his voice plain to hear.

Adelard brought up his brothers' life signs. The temper of a crusader was short. Elevated heartbeats were a useful telltale. They pulsed quickly, but not as yet with the frantic rhythms of rage.

'Forgemaster Dolus, what progress?' he said.

'There is extensive systems degradation throughout. The machine-spirits are sluggish. It will take many prayers to both the Emperor and the Emperor-as-Omnissiah to bring them to full effectiveness.'

'Twice the prayers, twice the time,' said Mallas.

'It is a holy vessel, brother,' said Dolus. *'Holier than most. I will wake them, make no mistake. This task is not beyond the skills of the forge. But be warned, repairs must be made to the craft's power net. Many sectors will remain without one or more critical systems until this can be done.'*

'We have gravity here and air, though it is foul,' said Adelard.

'And in the next you might find light, but no gravity and no air. I shall do what I can to ease your passage. Wait.'

Dolus shifted his communications channel. Binaric cant squealed over the vox-net as he conversed with one of his Techmarines. Chanting, flattened by electronic transmission, came with it.

'We have progress,' said Dolus.

Lights sputtered on in the nave-way. Ancient lumen globes burst in showers of white sparks as energy flowed into them after long absence. The Sword Brethren raised their weapons instinctively.

Fewer than half the globes lit up, most of the others strobing on the edge of malfunction. The lights hid more than they revealed. The nave-way was too monstrous to illuminate. Shadows shrank back to either side of the columned aisles, but refused to retreat further.

A chime drew Adelard's attention to an icon in his helm.

'Interesting,' he said. 'Dolus's efforts show us the way. A power spike – functional systems.' He gestured with his hammer. 'Come.'

A DOOR SET into a three-layered frame, all carved with saints and heroes, let them into the inner part of the ship. It opened, protesting, but it opened. Fresher air gusted out around it with a moan that died as the pressure equalised.

'Power, gravity, air,' said Adelard. 'Can you see this, forgemaster?'

'I can, castellan. If you will excuse me, I will use your squad-link as a carrier so that I might approach the machine-spirits here. You will experience a twelve per cent drop in efficiency.'

'Let it be done,' said Adelard.

A faint buzz came onto the channel as Dolus co-opted their suits' capabilities.

They were in a corridor five metres wide: a cramped space after the vastness of the nave-way. Pointed arches made up the ceiling. The lights up there no longer functioned, and so the corridor was lit by tapers of filthy tallow set atop skulls mounted on the wall. Stalactites of fat hung from dead chins, soot staining the walls above them. Detritus choked the floor – rags of cloth, broken machines, holy objects and bones.

So many bones. A carpet of them, ankle deep, that the Terminators' heavy boots burst into powder.

'What happened here?' said Godwin. 'The faithful, butchered!'

The Sword Brothers spoke quiet prayers for the souls of the departed.

'There must be thousands of dead here,' said Ercus, playing his suit-lamps further down the corridor.

'Can you hear something?' asked Rolan.

'Yes, brother,' said Mallas. 'Singing?'

Adelard concentrated. His suit's aural sensors increased the gain, sifting through near inaudible sounds. He caught it too. 'A hymnal?'

'Perhaps they have not all perished after all,' said Ercus. 'Perhaps Morholt was right, and the vessel was protected. Praise be to the Golden Throne if so!'

Godwin panned his suit-lamps down at the floor, having to lean his entire torso forward to do so – a graceless movement in Terminator plate. 'Your first guess was better,' he said. 'Look.'

Amidst the bones, Godwin's lamps picked out a horror; a skull, not entirely human. Although the bones of its face bore the features of the children of Terra, it grew knobbled and brutish towards the occiput.

'See, genestealers,' said Ercus, unable to keep self-satisfaction from his voice.

Rolan clicked the vox once, too annoyed to vocalise his acknowledgement.

The Sword Brothers' equipment whined as they initiated combat protocols, bringing their suits' machine-spirits to full awareness. Adelard savoured the angry pulsing of his battleplate's power systems.

Weapons raised, they followed the source of the song.

Increasing signs of disturbance showed in the muck of the

floor, signs of life aboard the dead ship. Skeletons clad still in scraps of flesh, black sinews holding them in postures with some semblance of life, sat against the walls. Priceless artefacts were mixed carelessly in with the wrack of ages.

The candles increased in number, burning brighter and higher, great plaques of solid fat flowing down to the floor from each. The Terminators did not need to sample the material to know what it would be derived from.

A door. They entered.

In a chapel layered with three centuries of filth, the faithful prayed. They sang songs in snarling, wordless voices, broken hymns to the glory of the Emperor, Lord of all Mankind. What appeared to be a man stood in the pulpit. He gripped its sides in fervour as he sang along with his flock. He stopped as soon as he saw Adelard enter.

The singing faltered as the Black Templars' suit-lamps stabbed across the chapel. It was a misshapen congregation, hunched and filthy. Desperate, mongrel faces – human but grotesque with alien admixture, turned to face them, yellow eyes set either side of pug-noses, rows of pointed teeth that caged black tongues. The Terminators forced their way within unopposed, Ercus turning outward to cover the corridor.

'In the name of the Holy Emperor of Man, I reclaim this sacred vessel for the Adeptus Ministorum!'

The preacher spoke. 'How can you reclaim that which has not been lost? We are the faithful of the Emperor, we keep his ship for him. We are his pilgrims. We bring enlightenment to those in darkness, we bring vision to those who cannot see. Who are you to say otherwise?'

Adelard privately voxed his squad. 'Stay ready. Do not attack. We can learn here.'

'Servants and worshippers of the divine Lord of Man, as you also claim to be,' he said aloud, his voice grating through his vox-grille. 'Space Marines of the Black Templars Chapter, the chosen knights of the Emperor.'

The man leaned across his pulpit, his neck flexing far more than it had any right to do.

'You lie!' he hissed, his face becoming bestial. 'You are intruders. You are the servants of darkness, decked in shadow. You have come here to destroy us!'

Adelard grunted in the affirmative. The noise was loud and hard. 'So be it.'

The creatures attacked as one, their movements eerily coordinated. Filthy rags were cast off to reveal twisted human torsos, though many sported additional limbs, all knobbled and ridged with xenos bone structure. In some, it pushed through pale skin to form hard exoskeletons. Their crooked legs propelled them quickly, and they were upon the Sword Brethren in a second.

'Destroy them, destroy them!' shouted the mongrel preacher. 'They are not servants of the Emperor, they do not carry his light within! Can you not feel it? Their souls are dark!'

Adelard bashed outwards with his storm shield, to give his hammer room to swing. Four of the mutant things were caught by his swipe and sent sprawling into their comrades. His hammerhead boomed with released thunder as he pulverised the chest of the first to rise, plastering his surcoat and armour with blood. The others scuttled away, tangling with their fellows, all of them growling and snapping like dogs. Most had no true power of speech.

'Slay them! Kill them! Cleanse the chapel!' shouted Adelard. 'No pity. No remorse. No fear!'

The chapel echoed with the howls of dying hybrids. Disruption fields banged and crackled as they shattered flesh. Rolan pushed his way forward, releasing fire from his heavy flamer. Creatures burned and squealed. In the half second the Terminators' auto-senses took to compensate for the roar of heat and light, the creatures had turned tail. Mallas clanged after them into the flames, but they were quick, and rapidly gone.

Injured worshippers mewled on the floor, trying to get up on broken limbs.

'Kill them all,' said Adelard.

'Suffer not the unclean to live,' his brothers intoned in response.

Adelard strode forwards. The preacher stood still, defiant in his pulpit, uncaring of the flames that burned the filthy hangings on the walls around him. An altar lay behind him, stacked high with bones – sacrifices to their unholy vision of the Emperor.

'We bring light to the darkness,' said Adelard. Close by, it was clear that the man was not a man at all, but a half-breed like his congregation. His alien parentage was there to see, in the ridges over his nose, in the total hairlessness of his skin. 'Take me to your Emperor, so that we might bring our light to him.'

The preacher glared hatred at Adelard. He smiled, revealing crooked, dirty teeth. 'Gladly, brother. Then it shall be *you* who is baptised, and you will feel his light within.' His alien eyes flicked down to Adelard's lantern of faith, hanging from chains at his belt. 'The true light.'

The preacher stepped down from his pulpit. He walked calmly from the chapel through a side door. The Terminators had to stoop in their haste to follow him.

'He is leading us into ambush,' Mallus warned.

'Yes,' said Adelard.

The not-man took them into a catacomb, a huge space dominated by mighty piles of bones. The dead were stacked, artfully arranged in tall pyramidal cairns, patterns in their sides made from the long bones and ribs, pelvises and skulls at the top.

These were the true worshippers of the Emperor, interred here as a mark of their devotion, and their resting place had been defiled.

A wide space had been cleared towards the middle of the chamber, the bone-piles pushed over and scattered. A rough nest had been made at the centre, bones restacked in the crude semblance of a chair. Fragments of gold leaf had been draped over it, torn from holy books, devices, monuments and the costumes of holy men. In this cradle of bone and treasure squatted an alien beast of immeasurable age and size. Two sets of gangly arms – one bearing wide, veined hands and the other triple claws – were crossed over its chest. Its carapace of alien chitin was dark, dark red, its skin pallid white and riven with crevices like bark.

'The Emperor of Mankind,' said the not-man in tones of hushed reverence. 'The lord of the Imperium upon his golden throne.' The preacher bowed, his alien eyes blazing.

Adelard killed him first, obliterating his deformed skull with one mighty blow.

'Here is the heart of the infestation. Kill it!' he roared. 'Gird your souls, brothers, for such as he are mighty witches!'

'Abhor the witch!' his warriors shouted.

The ancient genestealer scrambled to its feet. From the

shadows, from atop the bone stacks, more of its kind came. Dozens of purestrains, although none had the great size of their lord, nor the malicious intelligence that glittered in its hateful gaze.

The broodlord clacked its black teeth. Adelard felt a pressure in his mind.

He pushed back, drawing upon his faith in the Emperor. *'Do not let me falter, lord. Do not let me fail!'* he prayed. He tasted blood at the back of his mouth. His limbs trembled. With a mighty effort, he heaved the invidious presence of the creature from his soul. 'Back! Back! Back! In the name of Emperor!' he shouted. He waded forward, his giant boots snagging on the snarl of bones. The broodlord waited for him, staring malevolently all the while.

Rolan doused the catacomb in fire, filling the air with the sharp stink of burning bone. Ercus duelled with a pair of genestealers, his claws blocking their impossibly quick attacks. Godwin struck a creature aside, sending it staggering, dark blood pumping from its shattered carapace. Mallas slew one that launched itself at him from atop a bone heap, impaling it in mid-air and flinging it to the side. He pivoted, chopping another in half with one blow. A third died as it reached for him, then two more leapt forth, and he staggered backwards under their weight. Ercus, galvanised by his brother's peril, gutted one of the two trapping him, knocking the other away with a backhand swing. He reached Mallas, killing one of the creatures scraping at his armour, only to be forced to turn and defend himself from three more.

Godwin, meanwhile, waded methodically forwards and away from Rolan. With waves of fire to protect his back, Godwin was free to wield his thunder hammer to the fore.

His shield crackled time and again as he shoved away screaming genestealers. He wasted no movement, applying his hammer only when he had a clear opening. The thunderous detonations of its power field dominated the cacophony of battle. The brothers shouted with the joy of the fight. Mallas began the Imperator Exultis, and the others joined him in song.

Adelard cursed. The bone field was deep, a check even upon the might of Terminator armour. An angry bark of pain broke through the Sword Brothers' hymn. A spike in Rolan's vitals indicated that he had been injured, but then a deafening bang sounded as his power fist found his assailant. Flesh pattered down.

But Adelard could spare no attention to Rolan's plight, nor would he. A worthy foe awaited him, and he was eager to test his mettle against it.

'I am Adelard, castellan of the Black Templars, knight of the Emperor of Terra.' He levelled his hammer at the broodlord. 'I challenge you.'

The broodlord cocked its bulbous head to one side. A growl that could have been a laugh twisted its hideous features further. It stood tall, towering over the Space Marine. Adelard adopted a defensive stance, crouching behind his storm shield.

The broodlord swung at him, its claws a blur. Adelard blocked them with his shield, energy sparking angrily at the impact. He swung for the creature, but it sidestepped his blow easily, its inhuman reflexes more than a match for his. Grasping hands lunged, grabbing at his shield. One slid free, but the other held, long black claws biting into the ceramite of his Templar's cross. Unable to move his shield, Adelard was forced to parry the next strike with the head of his hammer. His armour's generatorium hummed angrily at the strain placed upon it.

With a mighty wrench, Adelard tugged his shield free and stepped back. His feet were fouled by the bones on the floor and he stumbled. Aided by the inherent stability of the Terminator plate, he kept his footing, smashing the genestealer broodlord hard in the face with his shield as it came at him again. He blocked again, then again with his hammer. A claw came at him while his guard was open and he swung his thick shoulder plating to block it, grunting at the sensory feedback as alien claws scored deep grooves in the armour. He shrugged violently, knocking the claw aside. With a final bash of his shield he flung the broodlord's arms wide, opening the way to its face. He drove his thunder hammer upwards, catching the alien beast under the chin.

The hammer's disruption field reacted according to the ferocity of the blow. Adelard had put his entire strength and that of his armour into his attack. There was an almighty crack of artificial thunder. The genestealer's head jolted backwards. It screeched as its jaw broke, and went reeling towards the rear.

Adelard was merciless, pressing his attack.

'O Emperor, in wrath rejoicing at bloody wars,' he shouted, 'fierce and untamed, whose mighty power doth make the strongest walls from their foundations shake!'

One of the creature's abominable offspring attacked from the right, but he crushed it without a thought, carrying the swing through into the broodlord's upper left shoulder and shattering it with another roaring bang of his hammer.

'All conquering Master of Mankind, be pleased with this war's tumultuous roar.'

The broodlord swiped at him with its three unharmed claws in quick succession. Adelard blocked two, but the third bit deep into his right leg, bringing forth sparks. He howled along with his armour's anger and knocked a following blow aside, breaking fingers. 'Delight in swords and fists red with alien blood, and the dire ruin of savage battle.'

He grunted with effort as he sent a wide swing at the genestealer's injured side. His hammer whistled with the speed of it. The broodlord twisted, barely dodging the blow, but Adelard was ready. Performing a manoeuvre impossible without the fibre-bundle assistance of his armour, he arrested and reversed the swing, sending it in a deadly uppercut again at the broodlord's head. It impacted cleanly, the weight of the hammer alone enough to smash the skull. Empowered by the disruption field, it annihilated the creature's head entirely, showering Adelard with gore.

'Rejoice in furious challenge, and avenging strife, whose works with woe embitter human life!' he roared, as the broodlord fell dead to the floor.

Adelard looked upon the broken corpse.

'A prayer for the true Emperor of Mankind,' he muttered.

Kill counters clicked up in his helmet readout. His warriors did their work well.

The day was theirs, and with it the *Veritas Diras*.

HELBRECHT:
THE CRUSADER

ALIENS BURNED. A crescent of fires held bodies blackening, a challenge to the weird walls of the fortress some kilometres distant. Spindly limbs cracked and vile faces, elongated and inhuman, gave a low uncertain glow. The fuel, perhaps, or the air of this strange place – so thin and unwholesome, it was a wonder there was life at all – stayed fire's assault. Tongues of flame crawled and wicked as they did their work, no blaze from these mortal shells. Ruddy light, gold and amber, red and blue, marshlight, witchlight, not conflagration; as if so far from the Emperor's lucidity, here on the fringe of all, even fire had lost its ardour.

Still the aliens burned, if slowly, and fire's lack could not also be apportioned to the crusade. The Black Templars had fought well.

High Marshal Helbrecht surveyed his men, initiate and neophyte alike: faces set with doleful mien, their souls as sharp as their swords, whetted for the Emperor's service. Lines of giants contemplated victory. Motionless, they looked through the pyre's fell light, their eyes fixed upon the fortress through the flame. Tell them will alone would crack that oddly lambent stone, and they would stare until it cracked. Black and white armour bronze in the fireglow, their unmoving forms were as statues.

The time of address was upon him, a duty Helbrecht gladly performed. The crusade was his own, called upon his accession, to the Ghoul Stars from whence no expedition had yet returned. His would. Immense pride buoyed his hearts, tempered swiftly by humility.

This was not his victory.

He walked into the weirdly chill circle of the fire, turned to face his men. His cloak, so rich, swirled about him. Chained relics rattled upon his plate, parchments whispered out his devotion as they rasped upon plasteel, but the circlet about his head was tight. His badge of office, his reminder: who had raised him so high? The Emperor. Upon whose shoulders had he stood? Upon those of his men.

This was *their* victory.

'No statue!' Helbrecht called out to his men. 'No statue will here be raised, no memorial to stand as remark upon our triumph! No songs, no poems, nor tales of deeds, so mighty that they astound the ear! No roars of praise, no feasts, no drink nor meat shall we have! No hymns of valour, no sagas of remembrance shall be heard. Frigid winds on blue sands, the inconstant light of poisoned stars. These things shall be our witness.'

He dipped his head. Wind blew in cool curls from the jagged mountains away to the south, strange aurorae danced in cold skies above, their sickening involutions lending the peaks a height they did not possess. It was hard to look through those cosmic veils. The skies of the rim were endless black, the putrescent glimmer of the Ghoul Stars not enough to part the curtains of the night. And glad was Helbrecht that it was so; beyond their feeble cordon were endless seas of vacuum. No light in those great gulfs of space, excepting the embers of distant galaxies glowing lonely, impossible distant shoals in an ocean that could not be crossed.

He raised his head again. The muted crackle of fatless alien flesh consumed played chorus to his words.

'These things do not matter. Who cares for baubles? Who cares for fame? Let our presence upon this world be our memorial!' He gestured to his men with one hand, open palm encompassing them all. Some he had known an age, some barely at all. It was of no account, all were his brothers.

'Let our feet, steel clad, pressed into the soils of this alien land, remark on our passing. Let the bones and ruin we leave behind be our joyful hymnal! What need have we of plaudit and praise? What satisfaction in elevation above the faithful is there, that can best the knowledge of service given? For we serve the Emperor! His eye is upon us. His will is our guide and our master. When we triumph, he is well pleased. When we falter, he aids our recovery. What is the opinion of men, what matters the swift-passing approval of mortal kind, when the Emperor looks upon our deeds? No matter these trinkets of recognition!'

He slapped at his own chest, his badges of office clattered. 'No matter the laurels of victory, no matter the glories others may seek. We are Space Marines, the Adeptus

Astartes, the Angels of Death! And more than this,' he said, his voice dropping quiet. 'We are the Black Templars. Victory is its own reward.'

The Templars took their cue. Their shout was sudden and invigorating, blasting back the sinister silence of the lifeless world. Helbrecht nodded in approval. His eyes locked with many of those before him.

'I would grasp each of your hands in turn, and give you my heartfelt thanks. This is your victory, your day, your might. I called this crusade not because it would be easy, but because it would be hard.'

More shouts.

'Today you have fought. Today you have won! We stand upon the galactic shore, you and I, travellers halting at stellar strand. One day mankind will call these hollow worlds all his own, one day shall he set himself out across the gulf and bring the word of the Emperor to places unimagined.' He clenched his fist. 'Today is not that day. That is not our duty.' He drew his sword and flung out the point so that it transfixed the highest point of the alien fortress. Atop those sheer walls of glimmering crystal, no doubt they watched him now, readying their uncanny weapons, making their strategies in their unknowable alien minds.

'We have triumphed. But further toil awaits – in yonder castle our foe stand ready. They will not flee, they will not submit. We must smite them all, you and I, and purge this place of their evil now and forever more!'

No shouts this time, no roars. The metallic snap of weapons being readied, the muted whir of actuators coming to life, the thrum of power packs as they supplied vitality to wargear.

Helbrecht at their head, the Black Templars walked through the funeral pyres, and towards the alien fortress.

THE UNCANNY CRUSADE

The Eternal Crusader came screaming out of the warp, as deadly as Dorn's own spear. Warp energy boiled from its Geller field, fading to nothing in the face of inimical reality. The wound it tore in space and time was healing by the time the *Majesty* and the *Night's Vigil* caught up with their flagship, engines howling under the strain of keeping pace. Slightly ahead of them went seven swift escorts. As soon as they had achieved translation to real space their engine stacks flared, propelling them into a picket line ahead of the flagship. Yet even these swift darts were not a match for the speed of the *Eternal Crusader*.

Finally, unhurriedly, the dark grey arrow of the strike cruiser *Revenant* broke the membrane of realities. Its machine-spirit showed none of the eagerness of the other ten ships, and it hung back from the rest.

The *Majesty* was a heavy cruiser, *Night's Vigil* a battle-barge. Both gargantuan craft in their own right, they seemed paltry things next to the *Eternal Crusader*. A reminder of mightier days, the flagship of the Black Templars boasted the capacity to carry more Space Marines than existed in the entire Chapter. That it was so was the Chapter's honour and their shame.

The Black Templars vessels were black as night, save where white panels broke up their livery, as stark as mountain snowfields. The forward prow shields of the two battle-barges and elements of their superstructures were so painted. On the *Majesty*, round bull's-eyes marked either side of the broad keel vane. Likewise, the escorts were decorated with white prows or command towers. Upon these fields the gothic crosses of the order were displayed, the mark of the first Templar, Sigismund, and all of his successors.

The *Revenant* bore grimmer heraldry: crossed scythes and a baleful skull, that of the Death Spectres Chapter of the Adeptus Astartes.

The three larger ships fanned outward, escorts hurrying ahead, adopting combat formation as soon as they were clear of the system's Mandeville point. The *Majesty* and *Night's Vigil* burned their engines hard, barely matching the *Eternal Crusader*'s speed. *Revenant* tarried, coasting forward at half power, allowing a gap of one hundred thousand kilometres to open up between it and the Black Templars fleet before its engines ignited and it accelerated to match the others.

Onward they sailed, towards cold, gaseous worlds orbiting a poisonous sun. Beyond it was the long dark of intergalactic space, a wall of night in which isolated galaxies shone, so distant they were no brighter than stars.

The Emperor's Crusade had reached the last strand on

the shores of the great void, the supposed capital system of the cythor fiends. The last of the Ghoul Stars.

THE COMMAND DECK of the *Eternal Crusader* was as quiet as the bridge of a warship could be. Servitors mumbled repeated instructions to themselves, and ratings and serfs talked in hushed, respectful tones, mindful of their masters' silence. The Chamber Militant of the Ghoul Stars Crusade Inner Circle stood upon a command dais, offered out over the tiered ranks of deck crew upon a jointed steel arm. With them was Naroosh, fourth captain of the Death Spectres Space Marines Chapter.

They wore their full wargear. The Adeptus Astartes had their powered battleplate, while the unenhanced Serjeant Majoris Valdric, master of the Chapter's warrior-serfs, and Shipmaster Baloster wore ornate suits of carapace. All carried swords and pistols. Arming servitors waited silently at the edges of the dais with boltguns and other tools of death. A number of serf crew waited attentively by consoles in the dais railing. A ring of servo-skulls hovered overhead.

The Inner Circle had their eyes fixed upon the holo-display, a glowing blue ball floating over the operations pit. Three hundred thousand kilometres ahead it showed two dozen cythor fiend ships of various classes, several of which the fleet had been chasing this past month. They had no formation, no common orientation. Their hulls, so recently sleek, bore signs of decrepitude. They floated in the void, decaying vessels in decaying orbits.

A voice sounded from a servo-skull, conveying the report of a bridge serf in the pit below. 'Still no sign of anything, Lord Helbrecht. Enemy craft remain without power.'

'This is the ship we fought above the World Crypt.'

Sword Brother Gulvein pointed with an armoured hand. A serf anticipated his needs and amplified the view in the holo-display. 'Only three weeks ago it ran before us. It looks as if it has been abandoned a thousand years or more.'

A different serf spoke, his voice made mechanical by the intermediary of the skull-vox. 'All auspex readings are negative, my lords. No life signs or energy. Their reactors are dead.'

Helbrecht rumbled deep in his chest.

'A trap?' suggested Valdric.

'Let me take a strike team aboard one,' said Bayard, Emperor's Champion of the Ghoul Stars Crusade. 'I will learn the truth of it quickly enough.'

Helbrecht shook his head. Bayard shifted, his frustration plain for all to see. His armour whined quietly.

The High Marshal lifted his mechanical arm. His forefinger hissed as it uncurled.

Baloster moved to an instrument panel mounted upon the dais rail.

'Pick your target, my liege,' he said.

'That one. Vessel fourteen,' Helbrecht said.

Numerals assigned by Baloster blinked around Helbrecht's chosen ship. 'Master of Ordnance, have lance battery three target it amidships,' ordered Baloster.

'As you command.'

The serf's voice sounded from the skulls. His shouts could be heard far below as he relayed the shipmaster's order. Baloster adjusted the holo-field, bringing the chosen target into sharp focus. A strange-looking ship with an undulating hull, it tapered at one end, was bulbous amidships and flattened at the prow. Its fabric was greyish, with a rough texture, the whole being reminiscent of an insect's paper nest. This fragility was illusory; such vessels had proven difficult to subdue throughout the crusade.

A half second passed. A gentle tremor, undetectable to all but the superhuman senses of the Adeptus Astartes, joined itself briefly to the perpetual rumbling of the engines. A bright light from the holo-display bathed their faces. A column of energy stabbed out soundlessly from the weapon's batteries upon the ship's spine, slightly off centre of the vessel's heading. The beam struck the middle of the xenos craft and the hull glowed hot. A series of explosions burst along its portside and gases vented from its interior.

'Enough,' said Helbrecht. The lance cut out.

The ships' relative movements, slight though they were, had dragged the lance across the surface, leaving an ugly wound. Impelled by the impact, the ship drifted away.

'Response?' asked Helbrecht.

The edges of the breach on the ship glowed a moment. Debris cluttered threat cogitators with munitions false positives. They were discounted quickly, red icons blinking out on the holo-display.

'No response from the xenos ships, my lord,' said an augur officer through the skulls. 'No weapons fire. No defensive measures. No sign of course correction. The ship is drifting without power.'

'Again,' said Helbrecht. 'Lance batteries one through four. On my mark. Cut it in half.'

'Lance batteries prepared, Lord Helbrecht,' said the Master of Ordnance.

'Fire.'

A quiet screech trembled in the air at the discharge of four heavy lances. Their energy beams converged on the centre of the craft, slicing it into two pieces that fell away from one another, the stern out towards deep space, the prow towards another ship.

'Xenos craft destroyed.'

'Time to impact of that fragment?' asked Helbrecht.

'Forty-nine minutes.'

'The other vessel is taking no evasive action, my lord,' said Baloster.

'I say again that we board them!' said Bayard. 'There is some trick here. Let us undo it with our blades.'

'The planet awaits. There is no resistance as yet,' said Master of Sanctity Theoderic. 'I suspect this to be a delaying tactic.'

'Have they fled?' asked Castellan Ceonulf.

Baloster consulted his augur teams via vox. 'There are no signs of other vessels in the system, my lords.'

'That means nothing,' said Theoderic dismissively. 'There could be another fleet hiding behind the star, or employing shrouding technologies to cover their retreat.'

'They have not done so before, my lord,' said Valdric. 'They have always waited for our attack.'

'These are xenos. They are not above hiding dishonourably if it suits them. This is their last redoubt,' said Theoderic. 'My Lord Helbrecht, if this is not an ambush, the situation suggests to me an evacuation.'

Helbrecht's lips thinned as he turned over Theoderic's words in his mind.

'Then do we hurry forward,' asked Gulvein, 'in an attempt to catch them before they flee?'

'Can we afford to leave this armada behind us?' asked

Ceonulf. 'We will expose our rear to a counterattack. All this might be a bluff.'

'We could despatch augur probes – it would be quicker and a lesser risk than boarding,' said Jurisian, Master of the Forge. 'If they prove to be crewless and truly inert, then we will be free of the task of destroying them until we have dealt with the primary nest.'

The Inner Circle of the Ghoul Stars Crusade looked to their leader.

'We have wasted enough time,' said Helbrecht. 'Obliterate them.'

'Aye, my liege,' said Baloster. He passed the order on, then bowed to his masters and departed the dais, following the stair down the support arm. Thence he went to the main floor, so he might better deliver the judgment of his lord. Dozens of deck officers and servitors set to work, all talking at once, calculating firing solutions and organising target priorities.

'We should despatch deep probes in any case,' said Jurisian, 'and cast out a net of augurs. There is no sense flying into the system blind. This is a strange foe. I shall have the forge prepare autonomous servitor units. Whether they flee or lie in wait, we shall find them. Should I request the astropathic temple perform a scrying?'

'Do it,' said Helbrecht. 'As you say, we shall find them and we shall destroy them.'

'Praise be,' said the others.

Jurisian took his leave to arrange both matters. One by one, the members of the inner circle set out to prepare their commands for the coming battle, if there was to be one. Helbrecht was silent. He remained alone but for Champion Bayard, who fretted for the fight silently alongside his master, and Captain Naroosh, who stayed to the shadows by the dais' edge.

'Destroy the ships, find their nest – it is too late, your efforts are aimless,' said Naroosh, the grim envoy of the Death Spectres.

Helbrecht remained with his back to Naroosh. Bayard shot the Death Spectre a murderous look, but Naroosh was uncowed.

'Best spend your wrath elsewhere, High Marshal, and leave the thankless task of containment to my brothers. The cythor fiends cannot be vanquished.'

Helbrecht ignored him.

'Very well,' said Naroosh. His voice was leaden, weary. 'We are observers here, nothing more. With your permission I will return to my ship and await the outcome of your folly.'

'You have my permission, captain,' said Helbrecht coldly.

Naroosh bowed and departed. Helbrecht's eyes never moved from the fire blooming among the dead ships, not until the fleet had been rendered to splinters of semi-organic debris and clouds of glowing gas.

Still no reprisal came.

PROBES SHOT OUT from small exit ports set over the *Eternal Crusader*'s prow augur arrays. Square as coffins, they housed the disembodied, lobotomised brains of heretics repurposed by the Chapter forge as mono-tasked servitor units. With a steady rhythm they launched, until five hundred coasted in long strings on either side of the fleet. At a single command, their plasma torches ignited, accelerating them away on pillars of glowing gas. At a safe distance, they arranged themselves into formation, a network whose nexuses were spaced a million kilometres apart.

Acting as one giant antenna, they filtered the aether for signals. Faint messages sent by cultures forty thousand years dead were isolated and discarded. Alien chatter was hunted down, analysed and dumped. But space in the Ghoul Stars was unusually quiet, as if the entire sector held its breath in fear, and they found their target within hours, buried amid the thumping voices of pulsars.

The minds of the dead conveyed their findings back to the *Eternal Crusader*, ten light minutes behind them. They accelerated onward, until their scant fuel reserves ran out, the damned souls within having unknowingly earned their redemption.

THE INNER CIRCLE gathered in one of the *Eternal Crusader*'s many strategiums to hear the message. Jurisian activated the recording by mind-impulse via the nerve shunts of his armour.

An audio fragment played, high register shrieks that made unaltered men wince. The same sequence repeated three times.

'Is that it?' asked Bayard.

'This is in no recognisable tongue or code,' said Jurisian. 'But it was sent only a few days ago, and is artificial.'

'What does it say?' asked Ceonulf.

'There are complex algorithms here. I cannot tell,' said Jurisian.

'Have the monks look at it,' said Bayard hotly.

Jurisian's servo arms, folded neatly across his back, twitched in annoyance.

'You are the Chosen of the Emperor, Bayard, and by his

will you are included in the Chamber Militant of the Inner Circle. But watch your tone,' warned Helbrecht. 'Jurisian is wise and well-versed in secrets you can never grasp. Save your choler for battle.'

'My lord,' said Bayard. He dropped his head.

'You have, of course, consulted with Abbot Giscard,' added Helbrecht.

'Of course. The finest minds of the Monasterium Certituda have listened to it time and again. They also could discern no meaning. It is a multi-dimensional model. Of what, I could not say. This is not the science of the holy Emperor-Omnissiah – it is unclean, xenos filth. But I can tell you from where it came – the third planet of this system.'

The world in question hove into view on their chart-desk, blue and ominous. Screeds of information detailing its hostile environment ran almost to the floor.

'The outer gas giant,' said Ceonulf. 'It is unlike any world we have found the ghouls upon.'

'Nevertheless, it emanated from there,' said Jurisian. 'It was a wide broadcast, radio frequencies. Very primitive. I cannot say for whom it was intended, but it suggests the nest is located there.'

'Very well,' said Helbrecht. He drew his sword, that most holy relic of the Imperium, and held it aloft. His fellows bowed their heads. 'By the Sword of the High Marshals, Sigismund's sword, into which was forged a fragment of Dorn's own blade, I take the following oath – that we shall purge this world of our foe, and cast the cythor fiends out forever from the Ghoul Stars.'

'Praise be!' intoned the others.

'Let this world be designated 9836-18, the eighteenth

planet targeted by the 9,836th Black Templars Crusade,' said Castellan Ceonulf. 'Let us hereafter refer to and name it as Grave Core.'

THE FLEET APPROACHED Grave Core unopposed. Large structures were detected in the upper reaches of its deep atmosphere. No signs of life were detected, but little could be told, for the cythor's structures and the world's atmosphere defied the fleet's auguries. Cautiously, Helbrecht ordered his Chapter to investigate.

The pilot spoke. 'Wind velocity is four hundred and thirty-six kilometres per hour and rising.'

The Thunderhawk's bumping turned into a ceaseless shaking as the craft sank deeper into the thick atmosphere. Hydrocarbon snow blatted against the cockpit canopy, leaving greasy smears.

'Be advised, brothers,' shouted the co-pilot over the screaming of the engines, 'we will drop through several layers of differentiated laminar flows. The disparity between currents is high. This will be a rough transit.'

The Thunderhawk bounced hard. Engines howled as they clawed for the air streaming ahead of the ship. It tilted forward, the rear bulled up by the rushing wind. The metal creaked as the pilot pulled the prow level, wind and engines raging at each other impotently.

'Wind velocity seven hundred and two kilometres per hour and rising,' said the pilot. 'Hull temperature twenty thousand degrees and rising. Air temperature two hundred degrees Kelvin. It is cold, brothers.'

The Space Marines, locked in their cradles, said nothing. The Black Templars were as belligerent as they were religious. If many of them spent their time from launch to insertion in prayer, equally there were those that liked to boast and joust with words before battle was joined. But this was a grim undertaking, an especially vile foe. The turbulence shook their tongues in their mouths, making them grit their teeth. Instead they silently focused upon the divine majesty of the Emperor and the righteousness of their cause.

The juddering image of an alien platform was projected into their helms. The habitat leapt from the display as if it was trying to escape, the result of the augurs mounted on the gunships repeatedly losing their lock. Although the Thunderhawks were being shaken to the edge of destruction by the planet's violent atmosphere, the platform did not move so much as a millimetre.

The habitat swelled in the forward view. Similarly fluted as the cythor fiends' spacecraft and made of the same papery organics, the bulk of it was a thicket of branching tubes, intersecting each other to form a three-dimensional mesh two hundred cubic kilometres in extent. Large hive-like structures were embedded in this network. Straggling tendrils twisted upon themselves outside this mass, as if they had attached to something now removed. Flat platforms that resembled great leaves were situated at various points, all at different inclinations to each other. The structure was grey and scabrous. Growing upon it were citadels of crystal, their clean, sharp planes a contrast to the fungal roughness of the rest. These were hard to see, hidden in the folds and frills of the habitat. Upon other worlds Helbrecht's men had seen such glassy forts, although built upon solid ground. These had glowed with witchlight that danced in the stone's depths. Not here. These were dead, mineral tumours on the habitat.

The flight of gunships split, fighting to keep themselves from smashing into the habitat or each other. They headed for different areas of the alien tangle, seeking level ground to alight upon. Searchlights snapped on, dazzlingly bright on drifts of blue snow.

No fire came to greet them, no message. No shields were raised or warnings uttered. The Black Templars landed unmolested. One by one their engines cut out, leaving the howling of the wind unopposed.

Helbrecht chose a wide space, a near-flat leaf that intruded some way into the root tangle between two of the papery hives. The pilot put the ship down as close by one of these structures as he could, seeking to shelter his brothers from the deadly winds. The ramp slammed down. An inrush of atmosphere equalised interior and exterior pressures with a bang. Helmet signums chimed warnings to their wearers as the oxygen-nitrogen mix filling the cabin was roughly compressed and chased out by Grave Core's frigid, hydrogen-heavy air.

'Onward!' snapped Helbrecht. Fearing his prize to have slipped his grasp, his humour was poor. He shrugged off his flight cage before it had finished retracting and stalked outside, Sigismund's sword already in his hand. The fifteen power-armoured Space Marines of Helbrecht's command squad and Crusader Squad Victorious hurried out. Five Terminator-armoured Sword Brothers disembarked behind them, Sword Brother Gulvein at their head.

Wind snatched at them, buffeting even these potent sons of Terra. Caution overtook their battle lust. The surface was slippery with oily organics and frozen gas. Armour maglocks were activated but found nothing to grip; the ground was entirely non-ferrous. A barrage of sleety methane cut straight lines across the platform. Visibility was low, the wind deafening. Lightning crackled in the distance, spreading zig-zag networks through exotic gases. Plasma sprites ignited there, skittering like live things through the upper atmosphere. Helmet systems buzzed and fizzed with each electric blast.

'My lord!' shouted Gulvein. 'An entry!' He pointed with his power sword. The length of it sparked as snow was annihilated upon its energy field.

Helbrecht marched toward the entrance indicated – a vertical slit, far taller than it needed to be to accommodate the cythor fiends. A bipartite door, seamed raggedly down the centre, barred the way within. Helbrecht pushed at it, but it would not yield. His suit systems showed him a thick wall either side.

'Breaching charges!' he ordered, his words almost lost to the roar of the weather.

Two Space Marines of Squad Victorious ran to do his bidding, securing bulky meltabombs to the door. They activated the mechanisms and retreated. A bright fusion reaction consumed the bombs, most of the door and part of the wall. The xenos material fell away to soot that spiralled off on the wind. Helbrecht kicked his way inside.

Gulvein shouldered his way through, bringing down more of the weakened material and widening the breach. He came to stand by the High Marshal. Helbrecht was at the very edge of a precipitous drop, his cloak whipping around his legs. A massive space was before them, somewhat like the interior of a beehive hollowed of its combs. The edges were crowded with twisting walkways that led to randomly placed pods around the periphery. The centre narrowed as it dropped, until it was a few metres across.

There a small hole glowed with blue world-light, affording a view directly down to the planet's core. A crystalline structure hung from the apex of the building's ceiling many hundreds of metres overhead. Suggestions of ramparts could be teased from its confounding layout, but again the crystal was lifeless and smoky, lacking the flowing light-forms seen on other ghoul-worlds.

Hydrogen winds whistled through the Space Marines' entry point, hooting along the unrailed walkways in a near melody disturbingly close to the sound of a human voice.

The Space Marines of Helbrecht's group entered the chamber and fanned out. Squad Victorious took the upper levels. Helbrecht's command group fell in around their lord. Gulvein's Terminators stopped a short way from them.

'Castellan Ceonulf.' Helbrecht signalled his second in command. His voice seemed unnaturally loud after the tempest outside. Static hiss filled all their vox beads, as if the world growled in its sleep.

'*Lord Helbrecht.*' The voice that replied was not the castellan's.

'Forgemaster Jurisian? Where are you?'

'*About three thousand metres from your position.*'

'Are you in contact with the others?'

'*I have found Bayard's group. He moves to join my Techmarines. Effective vox is down to pitiful distances. I can attempt a signal boost within a few moments.*'

'Do you have any notice of the foe?'

'*None, my lord.*'

'Then we shall make our way to your position and join with you and Bayard,' said Helbrecht. He brought up a thumbnail map in his visor and planted a rendezvous marker upon the schema with his mind. The map skipped and juddered with interference, much of it coloured in hazy reds and uncertain purples. He had a firm lock on Jurisian, but the other Black Templars' locators skittered from place to place as his armour's spirits struggled to correctly place them.

'Brothers, follow,' he ordered.

THEY WALKED AROUND the chamber upon walkways that widened and narrowed without reason. Squad Victorious covered their lord and his veterans, boltguns sweeping across the great beehive of the room. No threat presented itself, and the Black Templars' frustration grew.

On the far side there was another door. Helbrecht stopped, his command squad and Gulvein's Terminators halting behind him. The door was as the other had been, an uneven shape sealed up the middle, rough and tight. But he found himself unable to judge its actual size, and when he examined it closely its lines shrank and warped without seeming to move. His sensorium pinged uncertainly. The heat outline of the door writhed with menace.

'This door. My sensorium cannot get a firm hold upon it.'

'It is odd in appearance, my lord,' said Gulvein.

'You see nothing amiss beyond that, Sword Brother?'

'No, my lord.'

'It shifts, as if presenting new aspects of itself to me.'

'I see it entire and unmoving, my liege,' said Gulvein.

Helbrecht looked again. This time, he saw nothing untoward. Frowning, he ran his sensorium feed back. Sure enough, there was the evidence: the door's lines convulsed in the recording. 'The mind might play tricks, Gulvein, but the spirits of machines cannot lie. What I saw was real.

Sword Brethren, excise this door from its setting. Widen it. If there are defensive mechanisms within the wall, they will not catch us unawares.'

'As you command, liege,' said Gulvein.

Three Sword Brothers stepped forward. The stark blue light of active disruption fields reflected from the angles of the Black Templars' battleplate as they smashed the wall to pieces. They battered with thunder hammer and chainfist until the door was obliterated, and half a metre's thickness of broken, dry material lay exposed to the air. They ceased as one, judging the job finished. A blizzard of fine fibres wafted on currents of hydrogen-rich air.

'It is done, my liege,' said Gulvein.

The Terminators' suit lights played about the interior of the room beyond. A floor sloped gently to some point in the middle, past the reach of the Terminators' lamps. Tessellated, pentagonal blisters covered the wall as far as they could see. Acoustic pings emitted from the Space Marines' armour painted a sound-image of a huge space.

'This room is too large,' breathed Brother Guthrith of Helbrecht's command squad.

'It does not match the outer shell of the habitat, my lord,' said Gulvein.

Helbrecht had already seen this himself. He overlaid the supposed dimensions of the exterior upon what he saw of the interior. There was no fit between the external contours and the internal. His tactical map jumped and shifted.

'This place is unwholesome,' said Helbrecht. 'Be wary. Be vigilant. I detect the corruption of an alien witch.'

'Then we shall burn it upon the fire of the Emperor's abhorrence,' said Gulvein.

'Praise be,' the Space Marines replied.

Into the room they went, ever at the ready. Gulvein's Terminators strode ahead, suit lights blazing, their lanterns of faith flickering at their sides. After three minutes, the cones of light emanating from their shoulders struck the far wall.

'This is beyond reason,' said Gulvein wonderingly. 'What manner of evil is at work here?'

Helbrecht walked toward the room's middle. The floor was rough underfoot, and rasped against the metal of his boots. They saw now that the chamber was a dome, five hundred metres across, the floor concave. The air was entirely still, the roar of the atmosphere outside absent.

'My liege.' Brother Eadwine of Squad Victorious voxed his master. 'I have found trace of the foe. Dead. Here in one of the cells.'

The reaction to Eadwine's announcement was instantaneous. All three squads went into a higher state of readiness. On their visor displays, threat indicators tracked upwards.

'Check more of them,' Helbrecht ordered. He strode toward the waiting Space Marine. Brother Eadwine stepped back from the cell. The fold of material he had been holding open with his bolter sprang back. Helbrecht grabbed it and wrenched it free. It collapsed into fragments as he did so. The lord of the Black Templars looked into the space behind.

Crammed inside, its spindly limbs wrapped tightly around its slender body, was a cythor fiend. There was the long head with a tiny mouth and no noticeable sensory organs, and a pair of long arms and legs, each with two more joints than human limbs. There were no identifiable muscle fibres in its flesh, which cloaked crystalline bones and was watered by a weak, benzene-based blood. But whereas the hides of those they had slaughtered elsewhere had been smooth and silvery, this one's skin was as grey and rough as the fabric of the habitat. A fine web of gossamer strands covered it all over, somewhat akin to the silk spun by worms, but sparser and thicker. Helbrecht reached out a burnished bronze hand. When he touched the flesh it flaked away, as friable as burned paper.

'In here too, my lord,' called another.

'And here.'

The Space Marines tore open more and more of the warty blisters. In most were desiccated corpses of cythor fiends, the life long fled from them.

'What does this mean?' said Gulvein. 'Have they slain themselves in the face of our arrival?'

Before Helbrecht could answer, a garbled message burst across their closed vox-net, cut off as soon as it began. Banging followed, faint but unmistakeable.

'Boltgun fire,' said Helbrecht. 'Ceonulf has found the foe. Praise be!'

'I cannot raise him, brother,' said Gulvein.

'Nor I,' said another.

'Then we must find him,' said Helbrecht. 'Now.'

THROUGH WINDING WAYS that doubled back upon themselves, Helbrecht and his men hurried, the sound of battle growing tantalising near then far again. Eventually, Helbrecht's sensorium locked onto the locators of the other group, and they made all haste to the aid of their brothers. They crashed directly through a thin wall, bursting into a narrow hall where Ceonulf and his strike group were sorely embattled.

Ceonulf's men were grouped tightly upon a bulge in the floor, Ceonulf at their centre. Four of their brothers lay dead upon the deck, with two more badly wounded. Boltgun shots punched through the air in all directions, blasting puffs of spreading fibre from the habitat's fabric.

'Where is the foe?' roared Helbrecht, casting about for their enemy.

'High Marshal!' shouted Ceonulf. 'Take care, my lord!'

The Space Marines searched in vain for the cythor, but saw nothing. The fifteen remaining men of Ceonulf's group continued firing wildly. A stray round ricocheted off Gulvein's armour into a ridge upon the wall where it embedded and exploded.

'Cease fire, castellan!' barked Gulvein. 'You fire at nothing.'

'Wait! They return!' replied Ceonulf.

Chimes rang in their helmets, warning of spikes of exotic radiation.

'There!' shouted Helbrecht, pointing to a space to the left of Ceonulf's circle.

Things that defied categorisation shimmered into being, intersecting layers of impossible shadows that flowed into one another in a manner that hurt the human mind. They were undeniably sentient, and hostile. They writhed through the air, anticipating the track of bolt rounds and slipping around them. Ceonulf's men let out battle cries and concentrated their efforts. Helbrecht's group spread out, surrounding the shapes and lending their own might to the fight. The creatures were caught in a murderous crossfire, but unbelievably they passed through it unharmed. They closed upon Ceonulf's group, then leapt amid the combatants. For the duration of an eyeblink, they took on recognisable form: humanoid creatures of pure shadow whose skins writhed with glowing marks. Curved blades descended, dragging trails of condensing hydrogen fog after them. Once, twice. The crack of ceramite being breached cut through the sound of guns. Two brothers fell, one dead, the other clutching at his neck.

The creatures slipped out of existence, all indication of their presence abruptly vanishing.

Helbrecht's men ceased firing and lowered their weapons in confusion, Ceonulf's men following suit a moment later.

'We were attacked fifteen minutes ago, my lord,' voxed Ceonulf. 'They appear, attack, withdraw. Four times they have done this. We have three minutes, ten seconds until they attack again, if their previous pattern holds true.'

'Have you slain any of their number?'

'No, my lord,' said Ceonulf angrily.

Helbrecht pushed his way past his men. 'High energy indications when they appear suggests beings of nought but warpcraft. They can avoid our weapons.' He looked to the floor. A single patch of glowing blood sparkled there, although it was hard to look at, appearing to be upon the floor one instant, then above it, then passing through. 'This is devilry,' he said. 'But they can be hurt. They evidently have form. What has form can be trapped.'

'Two minutes, my liege.'

'Graviton guns! Meltas!' Helbrecht ordered. 'We will see how they fare when they can no longer move. Cage them in bolter fire, bring them down with the gravitons and destroy them.'

An impromptu fire-team of two graviton guns and a meltagun were deployed to Helbrecht's instruction, opposite Ceonulf's position.

A minute later the odd radiation returned, starting a wail of alarms in their helms. A second after that the creatures returned, hauling themselves from dark spaces near the ceiling. The patterns of their bodies glowed a throbbing blue, green, red and gold.

Once again, the Space Marines lay down a withering curtain of fire. Watching carefully, Helbrecht saw that some rounds did indeed hit the creatures, but they passed through them and did not detonate. The passage of the bolts hurt them, for he saw the squirming shadow of their beings convulse and flicker more quickly. He waited until they had been shepherded together.

'Now, brothers, now!'

Pulses of force nudged Helbrecht as the gravitons fired. The effect was immediate. The creatures shrieked. The shades that made them were violently arrested, and they solidified into the forms seen before, though now they were wracked with agony. Mouths opened, wide and full of razor teeth. Long pale hair flicked across featureless faces. They jerked around, unable to free themselves. The roar of the meltagun announced the death of the first. Before the second met the same fate, Helbrecht strode over and plunged the Sword of the High Marshals into the creature. He gasped at the shock of the contact. A deep cold surged up the blade, penetrating right to the interface of his bionic arm with an intensity that burned.

Helbrecht held fast. The darkness of the creature's body ran like oil, fleeing from the bite of the holy sword towards the shadows around Helbrecht's feet. As if dragged at by some force exerted by the blade, this darkness was sucked back toward it, turning for an instant again into the form of a shadow-man. Helbrecht saw slender, pointed ears, a hooked blade and pupil-less eyes that blazed green. Then it collapsed into itself, arms, legs, head and all, compacting into a dense column of purest black that shuddered then stilled. All the light fled from it, the room dimmed, and the column ceased its movements. Helbrecht twisted his sword, and the corpse collapsed into a sift of ash.

Silence fell on the battlefield. The Black Templars waited tensely for a further three minutes ten seconds, but no more creatures came.

'These are an unusual enemy,' said Helbrecht.

'Where are the cythor fiends?' said Ceonulf.

'We found many dead, in a chamber near our ingress point,' said Gulvein. 'Maybe these things killed them.'

'The ones we saw showed no sign of injury, brother,' said Helbrecht. 'And this thing had the seeming of an eldar wretch.' He gazed at his sword edge thoughtfully.

'Then what are they doing here?' said Ceonulf. 'Are these then the cythor? They are of a different form, but I have heard of stranger filth. Perchance they attempt to deceive us.'

'No,' said Jurisian heavily. The Master of the Forge came unsteadily through a door opening onto the chamber. One arm of his servo-harness had been sheared off. A crack in his left thigh plate was bobbled by sealant foam stained with blood. Several brothers and Bayard followed him, his black sword smoking. The number of their party was much reduced. 'They are not the cythor, my brothers. They are their hunters.' He stood a little taller, one human hand and a limb from his servoharness pressing into the wall for support. 'Come, I have something to show you.'

* * *

'I came across this place not long after we spoke, my liege,' said Jurisian.

He had led them down a short yet convoluted passage to another large chamber. Within were thousands of corpses floating in the air at different heights and at no common orientation. Some lay peacefully, as if in deep sleep. Many others were contorted, terror clear on their faces. The majority were human, but there were many aliens there also. The larger proportion of the humans were not readily identifiable as Imperial, but representatives of cultures known and unknown. The xenos likewise were of differing types. All were united in death, but most markedly in their appearance. Their bodies were hollow, their skins transparent; they appeared almost as glass sculptures. They would perhaps have been mistaken for such were it not for the clothes, trinkets and weapons they wore, and the augmetics that persisted still in some of the more advanced.

The Black Templars – Helbrecht, Jurisian, Bayard, Gulvein and Ceonulf – gathered around one of the corpses. Whatever process the man they examined had undergone had affected only the organic matter of his body; the nerve splices of his augmetic eye were clearly visible in the bowl of his skull. This one differed in one other important aspect also. His remains were full of a marbled glow, blue and green, red and gold, the sole lit lantern in a room full of extinguished lights. Helbrecht pushed it gently. The corpse moved into a new position and remained there, unaffected by momentum.

'He is the last,' continued Jurisian. 'All the others have finished the process. They have been consumed.'

'There must be thousands of them,' said Ceonulf.

'Tens of thousands,' said Jurisian. 'And there are other chambers like this.'

'Then where are they, and what is this thing of light here?' said Bayard angrily.

'Give me your hypothesis, Forgemaster,' said Helbrecht.

'I do not believe the cythor are entirely of our realm of existence, my liege,' said the Forgemaster.

'This stinks of warpcraft,' growled Gulvein.

'This is not the work of the warp. The geometries of the warp defy explanation of any kind. If anything, these dimensions here exhibit a greater complexity. Many of us have noticed the inconstancy of the rooms here, the lack of match between exterior and interior.'

'Aye,' said Helbrecht. 'I have seen it for myself.'

Jurisian nodded, the movement accompanied by the faint whirr of muscle bundles. 'Though complex, the dimensions of this place are explicable. This whole habitat is an expression of higher dimensional physics.'

'Explain,' said Gulvein.

'The universe we exhibit comprises four dimensions – height, width, depth and time. These creatures are, perhaps, natives of more.'

'You speak of the warp,' said Bayard.

'I do not,' said Jurisian. 'The warp is separate, unto itself, another realm entirely. There are more dimensions than the four in our own field of existence. It is through these that entrance to the warp is effected, and how some of the greater mysteries of the Adeptus Mechanicus are realised, but these dimensions are not of the warp. They are as real and physical as the heft of your sword, or the roundness of your bolts.'

'I do not understand,' said Bayard.

'Imagine, champion, that you lived in a world of three dimensions instead of our four,' said Jurisian patiently. 'Width, depth and time. You would have no concept at all of up or down, as there would be no height. It would appear perfectly normal to you. But that would not mean that height did not exist, only that you are incapable of perceiving it. So it is here.'

'You speak in riddles. If such a place existed, I would be able to see it. I can see no flat world, and so it is not there!' said Bayard.

'I speak of the greatest mysteries of the temples of Mars. It is not given to you or even to me to understand them, but that does not mean they do not exist.'

Helbrecht spoke. 'You posit then a creature that exists as a physical being, not a witch or daemon born out of the warp?'

'Yes, my lord. These new forms of the cythor are as real as you or I, but possess further dimensionality to them that makes them difficult for us to perceive. Forgive me, my lord, but I am unable to elucidate further. This field of study is the preserve of the greatest of the magi of Mars. My only knowledge of it is practical – the application of these prayer-equations to the proper functioning of field generation and suchlike. I do not know sufficient incantations to reveal the secrets encoded within this man or this building.'

Helbrecht gestured at the glowing corpse. 'And what is this then, Jurisian?'

'These are remarkable creatures, my liege. A fine enemy, deadly and complex. This, I believe, is how they reproduce.'

'You speak as if these xenos filth exceed mankind in perfection,' said Bayard.

'I do not, for that is not possible. Their very nature is a sign of their weakness. Why do they trouble this place at all? For amusement? A weakness. To feed? A weakness. To breed? A very great weakness indeed,' said Jurisian.

'This is reproduction?' said Ceonulf, looking at the endless floating dead.

'Upon the seventeen worlds we scoured, we found no breeding population, no sign of permanent occupancy. Their cities were diamonds dropped on sand,' said Jurisian. 'Think of those worlds, brother, untouched away from their settlements. Did it not strike you as odd? When man takes a world, it is remade to his satisfaction. Many creatures do this, but not the fiends. According to the lore of the Death Spectres, the fiends come and then they go.'

'Preposterous,' said Bayard.

'Hear me, brothers,' said Jurisian. 'There are creatures of the water of many worlds who must spawn upon the land, and creatures of the land who must spawn in the water. Perhaps these beasts are of that sort – they invade our existence to birth their foul progeny periodically, then depart.'

'And the creatures we fought across the Ghoul Stars?' said Bayard. 'Limbs, flesh and blood. Not this glow of light here.'

'Temporary forms, perhaps. I do not know. I am no magos biologis, brothers.'

Helbrecht made an angry noise in his throat. 'And when the breeding is done, the creatures of the ocean depart.'

'Back to the water,' said Jurisian. 'Whatever that is for them.'

'And the shadow beings, they are some further manifestation of this?' said Bayard.

'I do not think so,' said Jurisian carefully. 'In some of the other chambers there are smashed corpses, like these, but broken, the glass of them scattered upon the floor.'

'A hatching?' said Ceonulf.'

'I though so too initially, but these here have been consumed utterly, and are whole but empty. The cythor's other form is of light – the creatures we fought are shadow.'

'Then what do you suggest?' said Helbrecht.

'Where there is a glut of prey, my liege, there are always predators. We came here to destroy the cythor fiends and we find them departing. These other creatures, the shadow-eldar, have come to feed upon our foe.'

'Ridiculous,' sneered Bayard.

'It is of no concern whether Jurisian is right or if he is wrong,' said Helbrecht sternly. 'Both xenos can be killed whatever hell-form they clothe themselves in. We shall root out the canker from this world, and purify the sector fit for the sons of Terra.'

'Praise be,' murmured the Black Templars.

'We should consider withdrawal,' said Ceonulf. 'Destroy the world from orbit. We can strike these installations from the sky with ease.'

'Where are the cythor, brother?' said Jurisian. 'Not here. To be sure we would have to annihilate the world. Exterminatus will prove difficult to enact upon a planet of this kind.'

'Do you think something as mundane as Exterminatus will destroy them, brother, these things that can fold themselves around space at will? We must meet them with blade and bolt, as our brotherhood has done since the time of Sigismund. It is the only way to be sure,' said Bayard.

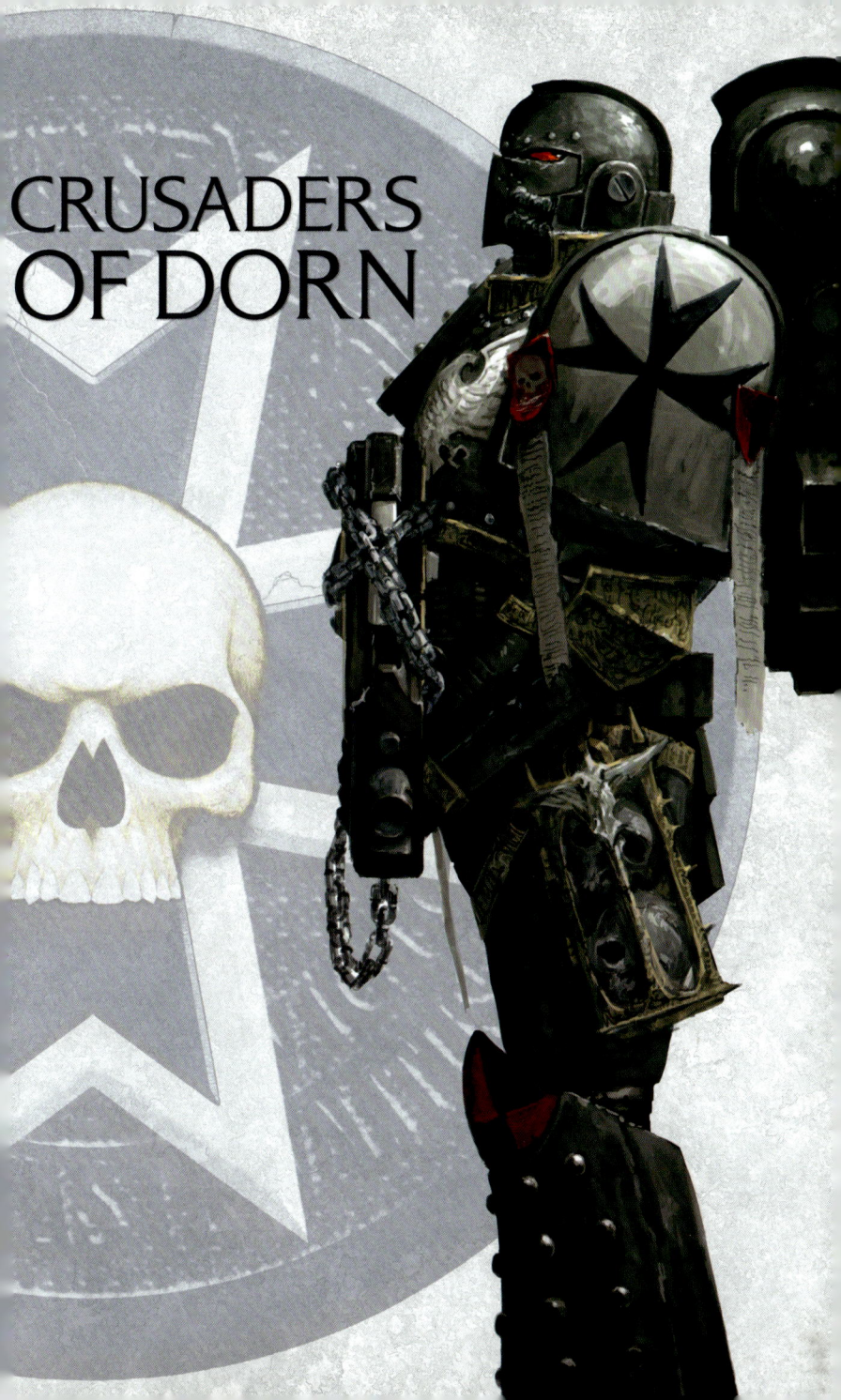

CRUSADERS OF DORN

Few amongst the Black Templars are as devout in their duty as the Marshals. Those who lead this Chapter of Dorn's Crusaders are fearsome warriors and even fiercer zealots of the Imperial creed.

'How long do we have until this facility fails?' said Helbrecht. He spoke tersely, his temper rising.

'I cannot say, brother,' said Jurisian. 'I have my brothers-in-the-forge Yoth, Skardus and Herl scouring the place for mechanisms, but if what I suspect is true, we would not likely recognise them should we see them. They may well be hidden from us. For what it is worth, there are hints of energy fields about the structure, and they appear stable in nature.'

'Monitor them,' said Helbrecht. 'I will order all brothers to withdraw upon your command as soon as you see signs of failure. Is that clear, Forgemaster?'

'Of course, High Marshal.'

Helbrecht clenched his fists. 'We must hurry,' he said. 'We must strike before our foe has fled or is destroyed by these others. I will not allow our glory to be snatched from us by degenerates.'

'Then we must find to where the cythor have gone,' said Ceonulf.

'There is an umbilicus, a root that goes down from the very centre of this habitat complex,' said Jurisian. 'I have re-examined the augur soundings of the fleet, my lord. There is a hint of something else down there, a little above the metallic boundary. Perhaps another habitat.'

'Then we go down,' said Helbrecht.

'My lord, the pressure of the planet's air increases a thousandfold. It is too great,' said Ceonulf. 'And the heat...'

'Terminator armour is proof against such pressures and such heat,' said Helbrecht. 'Send for mine.'

The castellan was not to be dissuaded. 'My Lord Helbrecht, to go down there is tantamount to suicide. Let others go in your stead.'

'Do not say to me that I am of greater worth than other servants of the Emperor!' said Helbrecht in a sudden rage. 'This is my inaugural crusade. I called it. It falls to me to finish it. If I am to expire, so be it. I do so gladly in the service of the Lord of Man.'

None dared gainsay him.

DEEP WITHIN THE clouds of Grave Core, a sister platform to that above rode out the ceaseless storms. A twisting stalk gathered itself from the top of the structure to wind its way up through the surging clouds, where it joined to the centre of the dense mesh of the upper complex. At that depth the pressure crushed the air to a hot, soupy liquid. The winds turned into raging currents. Downdraughts of cooler air and upwellings from further into the planet's roiling interior bubbled upwards. Down there was a core of hot ice, an intolerable country where diamonds rained on continents of hypercompressed carbon bobbing on viscous seas.

There, on the very boundary of a place where the conditions were inimical to all life, the fiends had their last outpost in the galaxy of man.

The stalk was half a kilometre wide, made of huge cords thicker than an armoured battle-brother and stronger than plasteel. Even so, by rights it should have been shredded, and it was not. The cord and the pregnant structure that fruited from it were still, untroubled by the liquid winds that spent their fury upon them.

But the Black Templars held that this inhospitable world was yet the realm of man, no matter that the light of Astronomican was faint there. They would not be thwarted.

Around the juncture of the root and the structure were

human artefacts, the shattered remnants of cybernetic devices. Only a few fragments remained, splinters of polished skull and steel, driven into the fibres that covered the stalk by the currents that had swept the rest of their components away. One remained whole: an extensively modified probe, proofed by the arcane secrets of the *Eternal Crusader*'s forge against the hellish environment. It had crawled down the stalk to its doom, but it had survived, and would for a few moments more, and that was enough. Within its armoured housing blinked a teleport homer, singing to the ships high in the void.

The liquid wobbled in the lee of the stalk. Bright light shone there. A shock wave of thin liquid burst outward. The Terminators arrived in a bubble of their own super-pressurised atmosphere, prepared for their transit, but despite the best efforts of the Chapter's Techmarines the air was not quite of equal density as that around it, and the returning surge of liquid hydrogen rocked them on their feet.

Helbrecht, Gulvein and four others materialised – Sword Brothers Aelfgar, Sotrnem, Giraldus and Leofric. They skidded sideways in the wind. Safety lines deployed automatically from their armour, anchoring them to the alien structure. Aelfgar reached for Sotrnem, steadying him before he could be blown away.

Helbrecht looked at his Sword Brothers, their outlines wavering in the boiling hydrogen fluid. His armour creaked under the immense pressure. Currents yanked at him, threatening to push him from the structure to his death even in his Terminator armour. His movements were slow, his strength waging its own war against an entire planet. Status screed redlined all over his visor display, numbers jittering only increments below the armour's utmost tolerances. He dismissed them in irritation.

Surging electrical currents made a mockery of the vox. He pointed downward. Giraldus hefted his chainfist, knelt and began to cut. He opened a wide space in the roof. One by one, the Terminators stepped through and fell rapidly, four metres down, trusting the might of their armour to absorb the impact.

They moved off to make space for their fellows as they arrived, suit lights flicking on to reveal a corridor as perfectly twisted as a rifled barrel. Three of them made a cordon for their high marshal. Aelfgar came after, Leofric last.

Inside the structure, the pressure was just as great, the temperature higher. But the vicious winds were gone, and the electromagnetic interference was zero. The tempest raged only metres over their heads, making the silence within sinister. Helbrecht clearly heard the soft breathing of his brothers over the vox.

'This whole structure acts as an energy cage,' said Gulvein. 'If it blocks out the signal of the recall beacon, our brothers will not be able to hear our calls for retrieval.'

The white helmets of the Terminators looked to the bronze one of their lord.

'Down,' said Helbrecht. 'We go down to victory or to death. It matters not. This is the path the Emperor has decreed, and we follow it until we succeed or die.'

'Praise be,' the others replied.

THEY FOLLOWED A long, spiral tunnel that looped around and around the structure. As far as they could tell, it was similar in form to the hive-like buildings embedded in the habitat lattice hundreds of kilometres higher up, but much larger in scale, and solitary.

Mission clocks clicked onwards in their helmets. At the appointed times, the Black Templars sang their prayers in honour of the Emperor. The rest of the time they said little. There was no variation to the tunnel: it went on and on. For what seemed like a day they walked, proceeding ever downwards and inwards.

After some time, the tunnel changed, becoming wider. Branches emerged all around it in spiral patterns, tiny at first, then larger and larger, until it became apparent to the Space Marines that they were miniature replicas of the tunnel in which they walked, converging on one point as rivers converge on terrestrial seas. The road they followed was the main path, or so it appeared, but they did not trust their autosenses, and half expected their way to empty itself into one wider, or stop altogether.

'Halt!' said Gulvein. By this point the corridor had become vast, thousands of subsidiary tunnels corkscrewing into the space all around. 'Movement!'

He pivoted his suit, moving the bulky shoulder guard from the hips. His suit beam stabbed out. A second met it, dazzling them.

Gulvein shut off his beam. They hefted their weapons, readying them for attack.

Staring back at them, from the curve of a fractally radiating tunnel, was a group of Black Templars: five in black, white and red, and one in bronze.

They lowered their weapons; the other group did the same.

'A reflection,' said Helbrecht aloud. His double said the same, the twinned echoes tangling along the convoluted interstices of the tunnel.

'They appear not to be solid,' said Aelfgar, and his double also spoke.

'Ignore them. It is witchery,' said Helbrecht. 'The Emperor protects us.'

'Praise be,' all ten Space Marines said.

They marched on, their doubles heading in the opposite direction.

The tunnels flowed together in infinite multitude. The solid phantoms became a more frequent occurrence. They walked round and round in spirals, coming stolidly towards Helbrecht's party, or going away, or heading down other branches. They saw tiny versions of themselves treading their own paths in the subsidiary tendrils of subsidiary tendrils. When they sang their songs of praise, the complex thundered to prayers reproduced a million times.

At first the doubles were exact, but after a time they began to notice differences in their doppelgangers. Subtle at first – unfamiliar badges, perhaps, or a different brother's name upon one suit of plate or another. These oddities grew wilder and more extreme. They saw themselves all in white, they saw groups of twenty or more, they saw themselves dead. They saw themselves in the yellow of the Imperial Fists, black gauntlets upon their armour. They heard vox chatter in their own voices but in languages that made no sense to them. They put all notice of these phantoms from their minds, concentrating upon their progression through the thick hydrogen medium that filled the tunnels. At all times the chief truth of ztheir creed was on their lips and in their hearts: 'The Emperor protects, glory to the Emperor.'

And then they rounded a corner, and they were alone. They were notified of strange energies by their sensoriums, and their threat indicators, red since their arrival upon the deeper platform, shifted to an even angrier hue.

'We grow close. Prepare,' said Helbrecht.

A CHAMBER MET them, wider than could be guessed or measured. The dimensions of it were all wrong, sliding from their minds as they attempted to perceive them. A radiance shone at the centre of it, a tall slash that stretched from floor to ceiling.

'A gateway, a tear in the world,' growled Gulvein. 'This is black sorcery.'

A multitude of shining beings crowded this brilliance. Their colours were those of the creature within the glassed man, but freed from their shells they took on shapes that were impossible for the eye to process – objects like soapy cubes that span about incomprehensible axes, or shoals of ever-changing pyramids. They orbited the light in a tightening triple helix formation that sank into its heart where the creatures were absorbed.

One form, far greater than the rest, hung over the light, its body playing complex rhythms of colour and shade.

'It acts as shepherd,' said Sotrnem. 'Sending them whither it will.'

'We have time if we are swift,' said Helbrecht. 'They flee our wrath.'

'For the Emperor,' Gulvein whispered.

'Praise be.'

They stepped into full view, weapons raised, their armoured limbs working hard against the liquid air. They were noticed, and the pulsing of the shepherd picked up tempo. The crowds of flickering shapes spasmed as one, the helix twisted the faster, and the transformed cythor fled quickly into the light, disappearing from view in a shower of breaking rainbows. The chamber emptied impossibly fast; what had been a throng that pressed every side of the room become a crowd, then a small group. The Space Marines staggered forward, guns, swords and hammers raised. They made slow progress, their limbs snagged by more than the treacly atmosphere.

There was darkness too in this luminous place – the blaze of the light at the heart of the room cast black shadows in the nooks of the rippled wall. From here, the predators came.

'Brothers! 'Ware!' said Sotrnem. 'Eldar daemonspawn.'

Shadows gathered at the corners of the room, black ellipses that rivalled the brilliance of the gate at the centre of the room in their blackness. From them issued the grim shapes of eldar-daemons. The liquid around them shimmered, condensed by the immense chill emanating from each. This effect made their forms waver, but they held true within their curtains of chilled air, appearing as solid creatures of blackness patterned with light, wild shocks of white hair around their heads. They wore no protection, even in the hostile depths of the atmosphere, but instead had long skirts around their legs that looked to be of flayed skin. Going in pairs, they stalked forward, approaching the edges of the herds of transformed cythor with sharded nets in their hands. Neither the shepherd being nor its charges appeared to notice this threat in their midst. The daemonkin stole forward and cast their nets into the shoal of cythor, dragging several pulsing, ever-changing shapes down to the ground.

'They have our prey!' roared Helbrecht. 'They steal our prize!'

At this outburst, shadowy heads turned quickly. Several of the outliers turned from their harvest and passed into places cast into black shadow by the brilliant light.

They emerged again a second later, leaping from the dark places close to hand and into the Black Templars Terminators. There were seven of them, lithe and deadly.

Sotrnem was knocked sideways as one of the daemonkin struck him. Another came at him, hooked blade pulsing with sickly light. Sotrnem took the blow upon his stormshield. A shock wave burst through the thick air at the activation of the energy field. The eldar-thing fell back. A mouth appeared in the lower half of its featureless face, hissing at the Sword Brother. He shrugged at the other, knocking it from its perch upon his pauldron. Both were quick, even in the dragging atmosphere, and dodged his hammer's blows.

Aelfgar and Leofric closed about Helbrecht, weapons ready. Giraldus opened fire with his bolter, catching one of the creatures in the shoulder as it poured itself from a crack in the wall. It was spun around by the impact, clawed at itself, then evaporated into wisps of shadow.

A third and fourth attacked Gulvein. He was wise in the ways of war, and stayed his hand till the last, reversing his blade and burying it into the sternum of one of the creatures as it came at him. The point of his power sword emerged from the thing's back and the thick air curdled with its black blood.

By the gate of light, the grisly catch continued. Dozens of the daemon-creatures trapped the ascending cythor in nets of shadow and crystal. Many more of them were attracted to the Black Templars, emerging from the dark places, showing needle teeth in mouths that vanished when closed. They came from the thinnest sliver of darkness, crawling down the walls, hands plunging from hollows in the floor to grab at the Black Templars' feet and greaves. Soon a crowd of dozens had gathered about the sons of Dorn. As they circled the Space Marines, they kept low to the ground, their movements as exaggerated and sinuous of those of a dancer. Close up, the glowing markings of their bodies could be seen as deep scars, cut or branded into their midnight flesh. All shone with a different light, this one green, another sickly yellow, a few an icy blue. The air wavered about them, a zone of churning currents where the deep chill that emanated from the creatures fought the pressure-heat of the room. The daemonkin's numbers increased until they brought the temperature of the chamber low enough for the temperature gauges in the Terminators' visors to drop.

'Come for us, foul warpspawn, and see what it avails you!' roared Gulvein. 'You have tasted our mettle – my blade yearns for more of your blood!'

'They will not attack,' said Helbrecht. 'They are craven. We have put the fear of Dorn into their hearts! They seek only to keep us from our prize. Well, I say – this will not pass! We have taken an oath to rid the galaxy of the cythor fiends. I will not stand idly by while my prize is denied me!'

'Praise be!' roared the Black Templars. Their blood boiled with righteous anger, and they threw themselves into the mob of daemonkin.

The watery air boomed with the crackle and banging of disruption fields. Ten daemonkin or more there were for every Terminator, but although the creatures crawled all over the Sword Brothers, they could find no way into the armour, and the Black Templars set about the glorious work of death. Gulvein slaughtered many, his sword moving slowly through the cloying air, but always to the right place at the right time. Giraldus brought several down with his boltgun, while Leofric and Aelfgar used their mass and crackling stormshields to force a path toward the fleeing cythor fiends. Helbrecht followed them, the sword of Sigismund jabbing and slashing into the packed mass of the creatures, slaying many.

The daemonkin drew back. Fell light played over their markings and a blast of terrible cold emanated from their outstretched claws.

The passage of the energy churned the air, ripping oath papers and tabards from their mounts upon the Black Templars' armour. The dark eldar concentrated their fire on Aelfgar. The blast caught him square in the chest, blazing against his eagle and cross where a thick sludge of freezing hydrogen formed. With a sickening bang, Sword Brother Aelfgar's armour collapsed inwards and he was pulped. On Gulvein's squad display, the pressure signifier for Aelfgar's armour shot into four figures and the temperature map of his suit became blotchy. He died instantly, his vital signs running flat.

'What wickedness is this?' cried Gulvein.

'It is witchery, brothers!' roared Helbrecht. 'Prayer is the answer! Devotion! Raise your voices to the God Emperor and we shall surely overcome them! Praise b–'

Helbrecht was cut short. Gulvein turned ponderously around, hampered by his armour and the environment. A daemonkin leapt at him. He thrust it aside, intent on his lord.

He was just in time to see Helbrecht be pulled through a dark shadow in the floor. The High Marshal vanished.

'Helbrecht! The High Marshal! The High Marshal is taken!'

With a great shout of anger, the Black Templars stepped up their attack.

HELBRECHT FELL THROUGH air no thicker than that of the *Eternal Crusader*. He landed hard on a pile of bones that shattered under his weight. Dragged down by his armour, he plunged deep into them, their broken ends closing over his head. The sword of Sigismund was jarred from his fingers, becoming lodged in the tangle of skeletons above him. His hand closed around the honour chain binding it to his wrist and he yanked hard, tugging the hilt through the calcareous mess overhead until he could grip the sacred weapon once more.

Bones exploded outward as Helbrecht kicked his way free.

He was in a cavern of black rock. There was no light except that cast by his suit lamp and devotional lantern. The environmental gauges of his sensorium flickered, confounded by the abrupt change. The room was at almost normal Terran atmospheric pressure, and a few degrees above the freezing point of water. Thermal imaging revealed walls of blocky, cruel-edged rock with a near-uniform temperature profile. He turned about, scanning the room with his eyes and sensorium. There appeared to be only one way in, and between himself and that exit were many piles of bones. They came from every creature imaginable, and all, without exception, were bereft of their skull.

Helbrecht shifted his grip on his sword and made for the tunnel mouth.

* * *

He did not have to walk far before he came across the heart of the place, a large and ominous hemispherical ossuary chamber. Except for a few black spaces, the rock was entirely covered with skulls, far more than there were skeletons outside. They were impaled on dark iron spikes, arranged according to species and size in bands and whorls that made subtle patterns. These became starker the longer he looked at them. A dais of black stone was set at the centre of the room, discarded skulls mounded up around it, the broken fragments of others carpeting the floor from wall to wall.

The empty sockets of the mounted skulls glared at a space someway off the floor. Perhaps as an effect of this, the entire space throbbed with sinister energies.

'A dark fane. I have come to the domain of the unclean,' said Helbrecht. There was no fear in him, no concern at his displacement in space, only an exultation of the spirit. Surely the Emperor had ordained that he come here. Soon an enemy of the Emperor of Man would lie dead by his hand. He gripped his devotional lantern and held it up. 'Come out, witch – I have been sent here by the Lord of Man to see to your doom. I bring the light of his magnificence to reveal your wickedness.'

A low hiss answered from the darkness.

'Revile the witch! Destroy the unclean!' bellowed Helbrecht. 'Suffer not the alien to live!' He raised his storm bolter and took aim at the skulls upon the wall. He let fly three rounds, and shattered a dozen of his captor's trophies. 'Praise be! Praise be! Praise be!'

He ceased firing. His boltgun smoked righteously.

'You make a space for yourself.' A low and sibilant alien voice defiled the Emperor's language. 'That is good. You are worthy.' His foe was right behind him.

Helbrecht turned just in time to block a vicious swipe. The sword of Sigismund caught a hooked alien blade that burned with the power of baleful technology. He flung it outward with a sweep of his sword, meaning to riposte on the return and end his foe, but the thing was too quick, dodging backwards and launching a flurry of counterblows at Helbrecht's head.

The thing was of the same ilk as the cythor's hunters – black skinned, pale haired, clad in skins torn from the backs of other beings. The cuts in its body glowed with a greenish ghostlight. But this one had four arms with skilful hands that switched the blade with flawless skill, making the direction of its strikes hard to judge. The sword blurred through the air, describing deadly, decapitating arcs, crackling as it went.

But Helbrecht was no ordinary man, and even among the Adeptus Astartes he was reckoned mighty, skilled at arms beyond the art of any. He matched the creature blow for blow.

This pleased the monster.

'Yes, yes,' it said, its voice a dire hiss. 'Worthy indeed.'

A blow quick as thought flicked out, scoring Helbrecht's armour with a bang. The Sword of the High Marshals sliced back in return, cleaving the air where the creature had been. As it leaned from the blow, its ragged fringe fell aside, revealing empty eye sockets as black as those of the skulls arrayed around the chamber.

Helbrecht and the thing duelled, neither forcing an advantage. They pushed each other back and forth across the chamber, Helbrecht's boots stamping the bone upon the floor to powder. The creature was quicker than he, but Helbrecht was stronger and far more heavily armoured.

The creature's only defence was its speed. Neither showed any sign of tiring. The daemonkin was possessed of unnatural vitality, while Helbrecht was bestowed with the gifts of the Emperor. He sang hymns of hate as they fought, yelling into the face of the creature's silence.

And so the duel could have progressed, the two locked in mortal combat until one stumbled, perhaps days later. But it was not to be.

The chamber rumbled. A deep, dark section of the wall vanished, and Helbrecht found himself looking into the gatehouse of the cythor upon Grave Core, blazing with light. He saw his men, free now of foes. Gulvein looked at him, his head huge and distorted.

'I see him here!' Helbrecht heard him say, his voice unimaginably distant.

The creature made a desperate lunge, a movement too quick for an unenhanced man to see, but Helbrecht deflected it.

'Hurry, Gulvein!' Helbrecht recognised Sotrnem's voice. 'The light is going out!'

'He sees us! Praise be, he sees us!' said Gulvein. 'He lives!'

From the shadows of the alien's lair an outstretched hand emerged, dripping alien gore and steaming with boiling hydrogen vapour. Gulvein was peering through a crack in space at Helbrecht, distorted horribly. To Helbrecht, Gulvein's hand was normally sized, but his head appeared monstrous, as if viewed through a flawed lens.

'Hurry, my liege! We must depart! It is over.'

Helbrecht glanced back, parrying another blow. His return this time caught the creature. It drew shadows to itself and flowed sideways, too slow. The point of

Helbrecht's blade raked across its ribs, only lightly, but such was the sharpness of the edge and the potency of the energy field encasing it that the creature howled in pain and drew back.

'I almost have it!' he shouted.

'Now, my lord, or we shall perish!'

Cursing, Helbrecht glared at the eldritch headsman. It laughed wickedly.

'I will end this duel, daemonspawn,' said Helbrecht. He reached for Gulvein's hand.

'And I will take your head,' said the creature, its voice soft and chill as blown snow hissing over ice.

Helbrecht took Gulvein's hand. Gulvein hauled upon him, and the dark realm fell away. Helbrecht's arm emerged through the head of a fallen daemonkin, bursting it apart. Gulvein tugged hard, and Helbrecht was pulled completely from the shadow realm back into the gate-room of the cythor.

'I saw you, I saw you in its dead eyes, a... a reflection,' said Gulvein. 'Fell witchery, but you are safe, my liege!'

Helbrecht was disoriented only a moment by the enormous change in his surroundings. The eldar shadow creatures were either dead or gone, their grisly harvest concluded. The bodies of those slain slowly dissipated into shadow, their white hair wafting on the currents in the liquid air.

'The cythor, did you slay them?'

'No, my liege,' said Gulvein, and there was shame in his voice. 'It was almost done. They have escaped.'

At the cythor gate, the last of the lesser beings fell into the light. It collapsed to a single point, blazing polyhedrons slotting into each other until it was gone. The shepherd creature descended, coming to rest fifty metres before them.

Things that could have been limbs moved. Light danced over it. It observed them as Helbrecht raged against it powerlessly.

Somehow, the thing spoke to them. Not with words, nor with the mental powers of a psyker, but in some other way that burst their heads with pain.

OURS, it said. THIS PLACE. GO. NO RETURN.

A shaft of light leapt from the cythor shepherd, playing over them. To what effect they would never know.

The creature regarded them for a moment longer. NOTHING, it communicated. YOU.

The shapes of its form folded into one another, the colours turning to reds that dulled to a deep glow, and it vanished. The light blinked out with it. The shadows lost their starkness. All life went from the structure, the confusing dimensions of the place catastrophically reverting to accord with the natural laws of the Emperor's domain.

The structure groaned. A rumbling spread throughout. With a lurch it fell, pulled in by the planet's enormous gravity. A section of it broke away, showing the raging, endless storms of Grave Core outside.

Pressure and temperature gauges in the Space Marines' Terminator armour screamed. Plasteel and ceramite buckled.

A ping sounded in their helms – a teleport lock, made possible by the destruction of the habitat. A fizzing sensation prickled their limbs, and they were gone from the world.

THE TELEPORT SEQUENCE cycled down. The instant the last translation icon blinked out, six teleport pods blew apart, burst by the sudden pressure change of their contents. Super-dense, hydrogen-rich liquid air catastrophically evaporated, blasting servitors waiting around the pods off their feet. Emergency klaxons blared as the teleport deck was flooded with explosive gas, great fans chopping noisily round to suck the atmosphere free and vent it safely into space before it could ignite

Throughout it all, the monks of the Monasterium Certituda did not cease their canticle for the safe return of the High Marshal.

As soon as the all clear sounded, Jurisian was out of his observation galley, limping across the deck to the shattered pods. Five of the six Black Templars were safe, protected by their armour, although they were tangled in the wreckage of their pods. The sixth, Aelfgar, was a crumpled mess of broken ceramite leaking gore. Small fires and explosions went off around the deck as Jurisian reached Helbrecht.

'Emperor be praised!' he said, his mechanical arms pulling his lord free. 'We achieved a teleport lock just after the habitats fell from the sky. What happened, my liege? Are the cythor gone?'

'Yes,' said Helbrecht. He held out his arms for his weapons to be unplugged and their oath chains unlocked by neophytes who hurried to attend to the battered knights. He wrenched his helmet from his head and handed it one. Sweat poured down his face.

'You were successful, then,' said Jurisian.

'No,' snarled Helbrecht, raising his hand angrily and clenching his fist. Jurisian feared a blow might follow, but it did not. 'We were not. My victory was stolen from me by others. Neophytes! Bring me my power armour and clad me in it. I must do penance in the Temple of Dorn.' He spat upon the floor. 'This uncanny crusade is over.'

THE GLORIOUS TOMB

THERE HAS BEEN a time of nothing. How long, I do not know. I know nothing when I sleep. There are no dreams, no sensation.

My first indication that my slumber is done is that I am cold and in pain. Praise be to the Emperor, for the pain and cold tell me that I live, that soon I will serve Him again from beyond the doors of death. Praise be! Invictus Potens is active, my glorious tomb awakens!

The cold will be fleeting. The pain is with me always.

A blinking cursor appears in my mind's eye. It is all I can see. Invictus Potens's eyes are inactive, and my own have not seen anything for five hundred years.

Words scroll across my implanted viewplate.

Cogitators alpha, beta, gamma, active. Life support systems awakened. He that giveth life, holdeth life. Let His grip be firm. Logos memorandum operational. Blessed are the recollections of the past, for in them are the seeds of tomorrow's victories.

Invictus Potens has a mind of his own, a bestial thing that meshes with mine. The logos awakens along with the logic engines that house his spirit. It will record my mental state along with his. My thoughts. These thoughts.

Initiate testing sequence.

There is a pause.

Testing sequence initiated. Engaging engine. Fuel pumps active. Ignition sequence starting... Three... Two... One...

A shudder rumbles through me, a sense of growing heat. Invictus Potens's joints move, motive fibre bundles tighten, pistons push against gravity. He stands tall. I feel the Dreadnought's movements as if they are my own, but the sensations are unreal, as if my flesh were numb.

I have little flesh remaining.

Engine test successful. Praise the Omnissiah! Engaging systems array. Engaging weapons links.

Invictus Potens's full systems array comes online in a blaze of coloured text, runes and informational dialogues that fill my sensorium. The date and time appears at the top left, chrono stilled at the moment my last sleep commenced. Targeting reticules paste themselves over the blackness. Ammo counts, all at zero, power levels, shell integrity, temperature, lubrication levels, fuel levels, elevation, air pressure, air mix, nutrient levels, amniotic status, biological component status, and more. They glow green against the black. His systems are hale. Beyond this, I still cannot see.

Remote activation sequence coupling requested. Guard the key, for the key is the gate. Remote activation sequence coupling accepted. Forge pass coding recognised. Identity coding

AA/LIF/ 5538 Dreadnought Chassis 'Invictus Potens'. Remote systems control granted.

I sense an intrusion from outside, a questing, electric presence that observes and notes. It infiltrates Invictus Potens's body. His weapons mounts activate and deactivate under this intruder's control. I watch the power feed graphs flicker up and down. These are phantom sensations. My tomb will be limbless, not yet fitted with weaponry for whatever role I have been woken for. The pain grows. I– *Argh!*

Biotic linkage error. Logos Memorandum interrupt. Reinitiating.

This is not a phantom sensation. It is growing, as it always does. It will reach a crescendo that is not quite enough to consume me, and thereafter become tolerable. The climb to that plateau is the worst part, and is not yet done. I grit what is left of my teeth. The muscles in my jaw are wasted. All of them are. My body is broken. Invictus Potens is my might, his strength replaces my own. His power uplifts me, that I might serve still. Praise be.

Weapon links functional. Weapon mounts functional. Weapon interface functional. Weapon power couplings functional. Praise the Omnissiah! Engaging auto-senses.

My vision activates, my hearing, my voice. Invictus Potens's augurs flare bright, whiting my sensorium out. I would blink, if I could, but I can do nothing but endure the glare until the view stabilises. It duly does. Grainy and imperfect, distorted as if viewed through a fish's eye. My sepulchre has been moved from my crusade's strike cruiser, the *Majesty*. I see the Mausoleum of the *Eternal Crusader* instead, flagship of our order.

I am free of the sepulchre's restraints. The oil bath has

been drained, the blast screen lowered into the floor, but I am still within the alcove. Not time yet, then, for me to march to war. This is an initial activation, as is standard. I remember everything and nothing. Only my thoughts are my own, only the moment.

A Techmarine and an Apothecary stand before me, clad in their battleplate. Chanting forge-serfs are close by, and thralls attend them. A Chaplain in robes strides the room shouting praises to the Emperor. At the edges of my sight, bent around me by the Invictus's wide-angle augur distortion, I see the stone of my grave, stained yellow by preservative oils.

'Invictus Potens! Awake!' declaims the Techmarine as he flicks scented lubricants at me. The Techmarines of the Black Templars follow the rites of the Omnissiah-Emperor punctiliously. I do not recognise him.

'I am awake,' Invictus Potens says. I have never been able to think of it as my voice, so deep and harsh: a machine's voice, not a man's.

'Praise be! Praise be! Praise the Ominissiah, who art the Emperor of Man in the form of most holy machine. Praise the melding of the flesh and the steel. Praise the Golden Throne, that which embodies this melding. Praise Invictus Potens, a hallowed reflection of our Lord,' the Techmarine says, his forge-thralls chanting with them.

'Praise be,' says the Apothecary, more quietly. The Techmarine looks at my casing, whereas the Apothecary stares deep into the distorting eye of Invictus, as if he would see me behind the machine's plating.

'All systems operate within holy parameters. Invictus Potens is functioning without the taint of malfunction,' states the Techmarine.

The Apothecary leans in to examine some device plugged into Invictus's front. 'Biologics read healthy. How are you, Brother Adelard?'

He speaks into the Dreadnought's ear, hidden behind the glacis. He addresses me directly, not the machine-man melding I have become, and so uses my old name. I appreciate his attempts to make me welcome, but what is in a name? Invictus Potens is my third. It is a label, nothing more.

'Pain,' I say. I hear the strain in Invictus's voice. The pain has yet to reach its maximum level, I know this although there is no gauge to measure it. The Apothecary nods and tweaks something. Warmth pulses through my wizened remains.

'Better,' Invictus Potens grates. The Apothecary places his hand briefly upon my sarcophagus in sympathy. His gesture is wasted. I feel nothing that is not directly relevant to the prosecution of war.

I think I recognise the Apothecary.

'What are my orders, Brother Hengist?' I say.

'What are my orders, Brother Hengist?' Invictus says for me.

I am wrong.

'I am Clovis. Brother-Apothecary Hengist was my master.' He hesitates. 'He died seventy-three years ago.' I have nothing to say to that. I have no memory of Hengist having a novitiate. 'I understand your error. I inherited his blessed wargear when he fell, praise be,' he says. 'The *Eternal Crusader* is en route to the Armageddon sector. An ork invasion, a large one. Many of our brothers have gathered. Do not rouse yourself overly, you will sleep again soon.'

I see activity behind him. Another Dreadnought – an Ironclad – is being exposed. Flashing lights over his sepulchre indicate his oil bath has drained. His sarcophagus door, marked *Cantus Maxim Gloria*, is sliding down. Incense curls around his grave. He is truly ancient, an Old One. This information is presented to me, not recalled.

'How long?' I say.

The Techmarine adjusts his bulky equipment. A new line scrolls across my vision.

Time check. Internal chronograph reset. Resetting.

The date blinks out on my display chronometer. When it returns, it is running again.

760998.M41.

Nine-nine-eight.

I have slept for 89 years.

Reset complete. Praise the Lord of Man, praise the Lord of Machines. Praise the binary of the twain.

'Eighty-nine years?' *Invictus* speaks.

'I am sorry,' Brother Clovis says. 'There was deterioration in your nervous system, a viral infection. It has been arrested, but it took time, and Marshal Ricard was unwilling to risk you until you were well.'

Marshal Ricard? I remember a Ricard. He was a novitiate, a boy.

'You awaken me now?'

'We are waking you all,' says Clovis.

Invictus Potens's engine deactivates. The power bleeds from his systems. The light is receding. I have many questions, but his voice is robbed from me. The clamps of the sepulchre reach out and grasp the shell of my tomb.

Testing complete. Testing complete.

Blessed are arms of iron, blessed are feet of steel.

'Blessed is he who impels them, though his own limbs

be shorn from his body,' say the forge-thralls, following the same cant as Invictus's systems.

Initiating mid-term temporary shutdown.

Blackness returns, crowding out the world. My vision overlay blinks out, the strength goes from the muscle bundles. Invictus Potens sags on his legs.

All that I have left is the pain. That never leaves me. Even as I slip into the dreamless sleep it is there. It is there now.

THERE IS A mighty clamour on the embarkation deck. Squads run to their drop pods. I see Brusc, for a moment, my last neophyte, leading a Crusader squad. It is he, I am sure of it. I do not remember how long he has been a Sword Brother, but I recognise his battleplate. Then he is gone.

Prayer, hymns and oaths vie with the noise of machines. Men kneel before Chaplains for the blessings of the Emperor. Ash crosses are smeared upon their brows, oath papers affixed to their armour by serfs with hissing seal stamps.

There is focus here, amid the clanging and the shouts, but an observer would see only disorder. Once each blessing is undertaken, the squad, brothers and neophytes mixed, leaps up with votive cries and jogs to the drop pods, another squad taking its place for prayer.

The last few of the pods sway in loading claws tracking across the ceiling, dragging them out of their armoured storage hangars. Chains wider than Invictus Potens's shoulders rattle as the pods are lowered into position over their launch tubes. The noise is deafening. Auto-worshippers recite endless prayers from metal mouths. Thunderhawk engines whine up and down, and tanks grumble into position. Loading claws bang. Sirens, klaxons, machines, servitors, brothers... All the holy tumult of war's preparation.

Apothecary Hengist–

Error.

Apothecary *Clovis* leads me to my drop pod. My feet are heavy on the deck. Brother and serf alike bow their heads and clasp swords reversed in front of them as I stride past. I am a Chapter Ancient, a living relic. In the honour of my entombing, they see an echo of the Emperor himself. It is an analogy I am not worthy of. I do not deserve such veneration.

The drop pod is freshly painted, bedecked with seals that will soon burn away. Invictus's name plate is attached to the front.

The *Eternal Crusader* shakes, under the tread of armoured feet, under the fury of ork bombardment, under the pressure of our zeal. This is a full combat drop. An armada of ork vessels assail our flagship outside. We go about our business without fear. The *Eternal Crusader* is strong and our faith is stronger still. The Emperor protects his son's sons. Praise be.

I enter my pod. As the ramps rise, one of our lay preachers shouts out our battle cry: 'No pity! No remorse! No fear!' He, like all the serfs, is armed and armoured. The lowliest of them are capable warriors. Such is our way. There is no room for weakness. Any who can bear arms are expected to do so, no matter their station.

It is silent in the pod. I wait. If it were not for my chronometer, I would not know how long. Time has lost its meaning, like so much else. I do not sleep outside of my hibernation. But I meditate, upon my purpose, upon the Emperor's will, upon the Endless Crusade, and I give thanks that I am still a part of it.

Praise be.

A chime, generated directly in my mind by the sacred technologies of my glorious tomb, announces the setting of the mission chrono. A second time count appears beneath my chronometer. It blinks red three times, counts down to zero, turns green and begins running forward. It is this alone that alerts me to my imminent drop.

A slight shift in my mass centre. I am moving into the drop chute. There is a burst of noise from the escape thrusters. I feel heavy, my flesh body moves in my amniotic fluid, and for a moment I feel with my old skin. The pain intensifies as I shift.

Only for a moment.

Acceleration is constant. I am falling through the atmosphere. They woke us all, Brother Clovis told me. An unusual move. Across Armageddon, seven of my dead brothers are marching to war again. Three crusades have been established. War wracks the entire system and a good part of this sector. The ork invasion here is of a staggering scale.

I am impatient to join the fight. I have slept too long.

The drop is short, and ends with terrible force. Again, my body moves within the fluids that protect it. I recall similar drops from my other life, when I was a man of flesh and blood. Then the blow of landing jarred every bone in my body. Now I am protected from the worst of it, numbed to it. I am distant from every sensation, and move as if in a dream. Only the pain is constant, curled around me in my tomb, intimately embracing my shattered body.

The doors blow outwards. Pale light falls across Invictus's metal hull. Ahead of me is an ugly ork fortress, an asteroid landed directly on the surface of the world. The land here is dry but not the driest – sub-savannah, low thorny trees and grey grass, all parched. A lush landscape by Armageddon's standards. All is caked with ash. The Season of Fire has recently drawn to a close. The weather is calming, not that you would guess it. The Season of Shadows has begun.

It is my task to aid in the rock's destruction. A worthy task. Battle rages already. I stride into it with great joy in my heart. Praise be!

'Praise be!' roars Invictus Potens.

Drop pods fall from the sky all around me, igniting the scrubby vegetation with their braking jets. I am one of the first, the spearhead of the Ash Wastes Crusade second group! Praise be! Fifty-six battle-brothers, forty-nine neophytes. Various armour assets are being landed further out, under Thunderhawk air support. All this and other information scrolls along the edges of my sensorium. Bright flashes and war-lightning show through the ash-tainted sky: the Void Crusade embattled in orbit. As above, so below.

Cantus Maxim Gloria is with me, emerging from his own drop pod sixty-three metres to my right. He is already firing, mass-reactive shells flaring as they accelerate away from the storm bolter slung under his arm.

I never knew him as a brother. What his name was is a mystery to me. He is and always will be Cantus Maxim Gloria, and that is how the other brothers see me. Not as Sword Brother Adelard, once-Marshal, but as Invictus Potens.

Am I Invictus? Or am I still Adelard? I no longer know who I am. It does not matter. Only the will of the Emperor is important. His will is that I serve. Praise be.

I seek targets of my own as I stride towards Cantus Maxim Gloria. Boxes and circles blink around the rock, highlighting potential threats, mission priorities and points of strategic interest. I determine a mob of screaming xenos, coming at us quickly, to be of the most immediate threat. Invictus continues to walk towards Cantus, but I pivot his torso and my sarcophagus ninety degrees to draw a line upon the aliens. By will alone, I discharge my storm bolter. The recoil of it, so slight on the great arm of my glorious tomb, feels sublime. War is the greatest act of worship, and I perform it gladly for our Lord.

Several orks are destroyed. The rest scatter for cover.

More drop pods are coming in to land. Fifteen are on the field. It seems all have made it down. Doors blow open and Black Templars emerge, covered by the storm bolters and deathwind launchers of their insertion craft. Controlled by machine-spirits, these switch back and forth with mechanical swiftness and precision, felling orks as my brothers form up for the assault.

The rock is seventy-nine point four metres at its highest point, an alien cliff-face dropped on the landscape like a pebble tossed by a careless giant. Steel doors and shutters cover its apertures. They slide back and the wide muzzles of ork guns are pushed out. Orks pour down from ramps and ladders, orks scream atop the battlements along its craggy top. I am surprised at how untouched the landscape appears around it. No scorching of the vegetation, no impact crater. A delicate descent.

Orks are remarkable creatures, a survivor race. I have fought them in swamps, forests, deserts, hives, snow, the sea and the void. They infest them all equally. Their success makes them all the more despicable. They are brutish, violent, inimical to all order and impervious to sense. I respect them and I hate them. I kill all the enemies of man with satisfaction, but I particularly enjoy killing orks. Praise be.

'We go forwards,' says Cantus. I let him advance ahead of me, to absorb the fire raining down on us from the walls of the rock. Six Centurions fall in behind us. We are the breaching party. Our brothers lay down suppressive fire where they can. It is not our preferred way of combat and they will be envious of our advance.

As we approach, I kill many orks with my storm bolter, but do not use my assault cannon, not yet. Its ammunition counter stands at full, a healthy dark green. Thirty thousand rounds are in my hoppers. A goodly number, but I will receive no more until the battle is over. 'The Emperor rewards with victory he who counts his ammunition', I recall a Chaplain saying. Which one, I cannot remember. I have known many.

We approach the gateway. Cantus Maxim Gloria's seismic hammer rises and comes alive.

I think back to the briefing. Three crusades, all bearing fresh names for the campaign – Helsreach, left behind by Helbrecht some months ago under Reclusiarch Grimaldus, the freshly instituted Ash Wastes under Marshal Ricard and Marshal Amalrich. Lastly, the Void Crusade, under High Marshal Helbrecht himself. We have arrived late to this war. We must pay for that with the blood of the foe.

I had never met Helbrecht before yesterday. I have the logos memorandum replay part of his speech.

'A victory is required. Morale demands it. Too many have died in this system already. The orks believe their fortresses inviolable, but worse, the warriors of the Imperium come to

think of them that way also. The Salamanders enjoy some early success, but we too shall prove the case to be contrary. Let the orks taste the wrath of the Black Templars,' he said. *'We shall not leave all the glory to the Salamanders! Let strike the true believers, the hammer of the Emperor. The sons of Dorn!'*

I hear he is a man of great temper and exceptional skill at arms. He seems worthy of his position.

Cantus Maxim Gloria approaches the door to the rock, wide and high. The orks build roughly, and this door is no exception. But it is strong.

'I will provide ingress,' he booms. 'Support me.'

His mighty seismic hammer sets to work, jerking forward, reeling back, bashing at the door relentlessly. The attached meltagun scours into the metal. Centurions join him, their siege drills chewing holes the size of plates, twists of swarf falling around their feet. I imagine the stink of hot metal. Bullets, missiles and many rocks bounce from our armour. I slay where I can, not a great tally here. The angles are poor.

A bright lance beam hits one of the Centurions, cutting downward through his neck into his body. My brother inside is killed, his Centurion suit locking his corpse in place. I have Invictus step backwards, tilting his torso back. I put myself at risk doing so, but this outrage must be avenged. Invictus's sophisticated targeting systems pick out the one responsible, a burly ork hefting some incomprehensible energy weapon on a jutting bastion above. For the first time that day, I let the assault cannon speak. The barrels whine and pick up speed. It is operating at optimum efficiency. The rites have been performed diligently.

A stream of bullets spark from the rock, sending gravel pattering down onto the breaching party. The orks above are driven back, and the assault from above peters out. I cannot see if I have slain the burly gunner. Invictus's readings are inconclusive.

The doors burst inwards with a resounding boom, one ripped so roughly from its housing that it forces out a small avalanche of rock. Cantus rips at the remains with his power fist. Then we are inside.

From that moment on, my assault cannon is not silent.

WE WADE THROUGH a sea of howling green faces, into a labyrinth of roughly hewn rock and abominable machines. These mechanisms the Centurions destroy. None can stand before us – our armour is proof against the crude axes and firearms of the orks. Cantus and I smash them down with impunity. We are surrounded, but that is of no consequence. Our mission goal is close.

Pain is my companion. The pain is constant, all encompassing. Death's legacy, a reminder that I no longer live, my gift from the Emperor and one I willingly share with these orks. A plasma burst from a xenos weapon ended my last actions as a Space Marine. I remember the heat of it, my flesh burning under my armour – agony, agony, agony searing out my eyes. They never told me, once I had been entombed, how much of me was left. We prayed, we celebrated, but we did not speak of my injuries. I have determined, after five centuries in this armour, that very little of my body survived. One arm. My upper torso. Most of my head. Perhaps my face still sits on my skull. Perhaps not.

The pain I feel now is nothing to the pain I felt then. But it is with me, always. I let it fuel my anger, I bless the bolts of our gun with it, it launches each blow of Invictus

Potens's fist, lends its fury to the spinning barrels of the assault cannon. This weapon, such a weapon! It clears corridors of greenskins in an eyeblink, leaving their remains to slide from the walls.

Warning. Ammunition at fifty per cent.

I check the ammunition counter. It is now orange. Fourteen thousand three hundred and sixty-one rounds left, but I cannot afford to slow down. There are thousands of orks here. I blow them to pieces, crush them underfoot, smash them down. Skulls crack in my giant's hand. So many of them die, die, die, but always there are more.

'We near the mission point,' says Cantus. 'Stand ready.'

We burst through another armoured door, into a large cavity at the heart of the fortress.

'Here,' he says, striding forwards. He is authoritative. I wonder who he was when he lived. A marshal perhaps? A castellan? He may have been a simple brother. Death changes a man.

The Centurions are behind us, walking backwards to cover our vulnerable rear plating. The systems array informs me that there are four of them left; where the other fell I did not see. There are many doors here. All of them are opening. Hundreds of orks swarm within.

'Activating teleport beacon,' says Cantus. The module mag-locked to his rear armour begins to blink with unhurried blue light. I carry one also, as do the Centurions. Multiple redundancy. We activate them all. It is a signal. Outside, the remainder of the Ash Wastes Crusade will be readying themselves, singing the *Pugno Gloriosa Mundi*, ready to rush into the rock.

There are over nine hundred orks in the chamber, according to Invictus's best estimate. Many are of the larger kind, leaders and specialists. I highlight these and commit their positions to Invictus's targeting memory.

'Stand firm,' I say.

The orks stand, staring at us, roaring at us, making their crude threat displays, but make no move against us, until one, a huge beast, moves out from the crowd and bellows a long challenge. It is taken up by the others, and they charge.

My assault cannon speaks until it has run out of words. Thereafter I use its red-hot barrels to brand orks with the mark of death. It is a holy mark, but no absolution comes with it, only annihilation.

A group of orks armed with large explosive charges and crude missiles come shoving through the crowd. I raise Invictus's storm bolter, but that too is empty. Red mars the green of my systems array – no ammo, overheating, dropping fuel.

They charge towards Cantus Maxim Gloria. I interpose myself to save him, and doom myself.

They are all over my tomb, slapping charges to its limbs. One swings its strange rocket hammer at me, but I catch him, engulfing head and shoulders in Invictus's fist, rendering them into a pulp.

There is a dim blue glow coming from the centre of the room. Greasy smoke smears the air. Shapes form. Marshal Ricard and Sword Brothers in Terminator armour step out from the light. Our mission is a success. But it is too late for me.

There is an explosion on Invictus's lower portions, then another. The ground rushes up at me as he falls. My tomb's pain arrests me, but it is feeble compared to my own, and is quickly over.

* * *

Warning. Warning. Warning. Systems compromised. Await aid. Fortitude is the ultimate fortress.

There follows a long list of damaged machinery. Blinking red text and runes. All I see beyond them is the gritty floor. I do not read it. I do not need to read it. There is another explosion, this time upon Invictus's back. Shortly after, the systems array blinks and goes out, never to come again. I lose my connection with Invictus entirely.

I am left in the dark with my pain.

My fluid is pouring out through the crack in my sarcophagus. Invictus is sorely injured, but my brothers will slaughter every ork that stands between they and he, even if the greenskins are a million in number. Invictus will fight again. I, however, will not.

I pray.

I realise that I can still hear the sounds of battle, the hymns of my brothers, the triple bark of bolt rounds being expelled, igniting, exploding. I smile, or attempt to. I hear with my own ears for the first time in five centuries – the final time.

I do not know what to expect next. It strikes me as amusing that I actually expect something more, that I assume the procession of events cannot end. That is why humanity is so indomitable. Even dying, we do not stop. Perhaps, as a race, we die even now, and my situation is analogous in miniature to the situation of every man, woman and child of our species: awaiting the next event, when there is only death.

I will never know if this is the case or not. I have faith that mankind will prevail. If I have no faith, what do I have? Defeat. I have faith. Even as I die I know victory.

These are my thoughts: What happens to us when we

die? Does the Emperor wait for me, whole in spirit as he no longer is in life, to call me to his side and sit with him at the table? Will it simply end? There is no golden light, no sense of impending doom, no terrifying sensation. No comfort either.

The last of the fluid has gone, exposing my skin to the air. I am aware now, of how little of me there is left, trapped in this glorious tomb. Things tug at my flesh, the pipes and cables of Invictus's interface. A terrible chill grips me. I struggle with the urge to breathe, but I have no lungs. The oxygen levels in my blood are dipping dangerously low. My skin crawls as my remaining genetic gifts, the Emperor's holy boon that made me into a Space Marine – broken things now – struggle to keep me alive. Too late, too late. The final journey approaches.

Consciousness recedes. I have felt little emotion since the day I was entombed. Pride, zeal, courage, honour – all come back to me as I die, and I am grateful to feel them again. The day I was chosen to become a Black Templar. My elevation to Sword Brother. My days as a marshal. The battle on Vellinus, the reaving of the Cemetery Worlds, the misguided Passion of The False Saint Cleon, the hunting of the Ork Wyrd. All ended in blood and death. Brusc, Oberon, Danifer, Theilred, Chardin... So many faces I have known, all going into the black. A million deaths by my hand. If not all were righteous, most were. I can ask for no more than that. Was it not blessed Artemisia who said 'Better a thousand good men die than one traitor go free'?

Older memories, long neglected, resurface. Golden light, a man's laughter. My father, perhaps. A rare moment of peace on my benighted homeworld. He pushes me on a swing, a rope on a tree branch over the only safe water for kilometres. I am shrieking with fright at how high and fast he is pushing me. He pushes harder.

'Be brave, Kellon!' he shouts. 'Be brave!' I shriek louder, a boy's squeals. He reminds me of how brave I am when the gentar reptiles come. I am already inured to death, already a warrior, but it does not prevent my shrill cries, a little fear, but mostly pleasure. He mocks me fondly for it. 'I have been brave for all my days!' I shout in my boy's voice. 'I have known no fear!' But he is a memory and cannot hear.

I close my eyes, I listen to that laughter. Four years after this I had no father, and no home, but that is yet to come. Such pleasure: simple, potent, and pure. So different to the holy joys of battle, so different to the raptures of worship. There is no aim to it, no reason – it simply is. I wonder what my life would have been had I not trekked to the keep, if I had not undertaken the trial. I think this, only for an instant, Lord, but I think it. Forgive me this last sin, O Emperor.

The air of my youth is warm but I am cold. A shadow comes, dimming the sun. My father does not notice. I try to get his attention. Still he does not hear, trapped as he is in the past. It is fitting, perhaps, for the past is all I have. The final curtain is drawing over my life. I have fought well, have I not, O Master of Mankind? My toil is over, and I go gladly to my reward.

Despite my faith, I am afraid I will not be heard.

But praise be! Thanks to the Emperor, he hears me! He hears me! There comes a last blessing. The cold recedes. I am warm. I am free. I turn to tell the fading vision of my past, calling out in joy to the shadows in the thickening dark.

'The pain is gone,' I cry. 'The pain is gone!'

++ Appended Black Templars Forge note, 987721/3/2 AA/LIF/5538 Dreadnought Chassis 'Invictus Potens' internal datalogue. Brother Adelard Logos Memorandum records cease. 'Invictus Potens' recovered. ++

++ Praise be. ++

ONLY BLOOD

'There's definitely something there!'

Brother Sunno leaned over to look through the open door of the driver's cab, shouting to make himself heard over the throb of Rhino's engines. He had his helmet off. The atmosphere in the tank was thick and bitter, but better, he said, than breathing endlessly recycled suit air. The four Black Templars in the battered passenger compartment, two novitiates and two initiates, shifted their gazes from whatever internal space they'd been examining and glanced at the forward comms panel. The novitiates blinked slowly, as if perplexed. It had been a hard few days for them all.

'Bring *Cataphraxes* to a halt,' ordered Brusc, Sword Brother of the Ash Wastes Crusade, commanding officer of this sorry remnant. He drummed metal-clad fingers on his armoured thigh, rattling out a brief, tinny tattoo in the Rhino's passenger cab. Near silence fell suddenly as

Sunno cut the engine. Small sounds grew large: the wind whistling over the tank's fittings, muted by thick armour; the almost inaudible whine of power armour at rest; the thunderous breathing of the five giants within the tank.

The communications array on the forward wall hissed unhelpfully, its screen set to seeking auspex and fizzing with green static snow.

Brusc exhaled contemplatively, his eyes shifting to each of the warriors with him. Osric, Sunno in the cab, the novitiates Marcomar and Doneal, not yet initiates, already mightier than fully grown unenhanced men. The tight scar tissue on his face itched as it always did when he was tired. He did his best to ignore it.

'Brother Osric? What say you?' asked Brusc eventually.

Osric frowned, stood, took a couple of bowed steps forward and slapped the comms array with his armoured fist. The screen jumped. Thick lines crawled down from the top. Electric snow returned.

'Are you sure you should do that, brother?' asked Brusc. 'It is not the manner in which I've seen the tech-priests address the machine.'

'Half of what they do is striking things,' muttered Osric.

Brusc barked out a laugh. The boys jumped at the noise, they were not yet acquainted with his ways.

'That's as may be, but you not know the correct preparatory prayers.'

'It still works, Sword Brother, and I've got something. Listen!'

'Fall bac... ...o sector 15... Enem... eeee...' The vox broke off into a cascade of menacing buzzes.

'The signal's getting worse,' grumbled Brusc. His good humour deserted him as quickly as it came. He was mercurial like that, as Osric well knew. It made others wary of him, but not Osric.

'The Season of Fire on Armageddon. What are we to expect?' asked Sunno.

'The Kannheim tower must be down again,' said Osric. 'The orks knock it down as quickly as Munitorum put it up again.'

'First the satellites, now this,' said Sunno. 'The orks are smashing every broadcast tower and mast they come across. They are no fools. We have our orders. Retreat, regroup. Give the word, Sword Brother, and I'll add more dust to this accursed storm.'

Brusc said nothing. The wind outside hooted. Storm-blown gravel pattered against the hull.

'What do you think then, brother? Do we investigate?' asked Osric. 'There's supposed to be a field hospital hereabouts. It might be that. Standing orders from High Command are to keep watch for stragglers. They might not have heard.'

'And it might be a nest of orks,' said Sunno. 'We are not subject to the orders of any but Marshal Ricard, and he said only to regroup. Let standard humans look out for their own. I say we move on.'

'Come now! A nest of orks would be well. I could do with wetting my blade, not sitting in this box day in day out,' said Osric with a broad smile.

That pleased Brusc. He smiled too, a somewhat hideous expression on his disfigured face, and jabbed his finger at Osric. 'Very well. Come on, you're with me.'

'Not a waste of time then, brother?' asked Osric, addressing Brusc but speaking chiefly to Sunno.

'Maybe, maybe not,' said Brusc, 'but if I leave you in here

hitting the machinery you're likely to so offend *Catraphaxes* that the Machine-God himself will seize up your armour. Sunno, stay with the neophytes.'

'Yes, Sword Brother,' said Sunno. He turned back to the Rhino's drive console, irked that his counsel had not been followed.

'Best cover your mouths, boys,' said Brusc.

'Yes, my lord,' said the neophytes. Already the veterans of fifteen battles, they still cast their eyes down and spoke humbly whenever Brusc addressed them. They called him the Old Man, and not just the neophytes. True, he was the oldest living Black Templar, or so it was reckoned. Perhaps even the oldest of all the sons of Dorn, saving Captain Lysander of the Imperial Fists, but it was not a name he encouraged here; there was another Old Man on Armageddon. Although far more ancient than Yarrick, Brusc thought the commissar deserved the affection and respect the name best represented.

He regarded the men. Five of the crusaders left from ten, a pitiful score, and a tally of dead he was not relishing relaying to Marshal Ricard. Marcomar had taken the loss of his master particularly hard. His knee jogged up and down, and he gripped his sniper rifle too tightly across his knees. By Brusc's assessment, Marcomar was close to failing the final stages of his initiation.

'Cover your mouths,' he repeated, more gently. He scratched his unnaturally smooth cheek then nodded at Osric. Both of them put their helmets on. Live displays burst into life across Brusc's field of vision as his sensorium engaged. After checking his visual markers to ensure his armour was hale, Brusc activated *Cataphraxes*'s door rune with a thought. He and Osric retrieved their weapons from the rack: a chainsword and bolt pistol each.

The Rhino's rear ramp squealed open, its mechanisms fouled by wind-blown dust. Brusc muttered quick thanks to *Catraphaxes*'s machine-spirit. He worried it might grow angry, and not only from Osric's less than reverent treatment. Few things made by man were suited to Armageddon's Ash Wastes. Billows of dust and ash flooded the passenger compartment, setting off alarms in the Rhino's cab.

Brusc and Osric stamped out into the dust storm. The sound of the alarms were lost instantly to the howl of the gale. They spoke the rites of awakening to prepare their weapons for battle, but they did not clip their wrist lanyard chains in place – not yet.

'Ah, I've got a signal now. Imperial marker beacon. It is the field hospital,' said Osric. A moment later, Brusc had it too.

'Any vox?'

'Nothing,' said Osric.

'Then we had better knock.'

The Black Templars were virtually blind, would have been blind were it not for the spirits of their armour. Blinking arrows and compass wheels on their visor interface guided them toward the installation. When they grew close to it, wireframe outlines sprang into life, giving hard edges of light to the shadowy buildings coalescing from the brown air. Only when they were close enough to touch the perimeter fence did the shapes become identifiable as prefabricatum units, the same as could be found on hundreds of thousands of worlds across the galaxy.

'As you say,' said Brusc, only putting away his weapons when he confirmed by sight what his suit told him. He apologised to his gun and blade as they maglocked to his armour.

'Are you sure it is still in human hands?' said Osric. He was as reluctant to put up his own gun and sword unblooded.

'Absolutely,' said Brusc. 'I see no sign of orkish defilement, no sign of battle, even.' They spoke via helmet vox. Their speaker grilles were full of sand, any words spat out of them snatched away by the ferocious wind. The rattle of pumice and sand against their helmets was so loud, they were forced nearly to shout.

Osric did as Brusc had, attaching his chainsword to his left hip, his bolt pistol to his right. 'We'll be lucky to get close without them shooting us,' said Osric.

'They'll be lucky to survive if they do,' said Brusc. The storm put him in a poor mood, and he was only half-joking.

They followed the edge of the perimeter, a segmented, plascrete defence line losing its feet in the ash. 'No one about,' said Brusc. 'Sloppy.'

'Not even the orks are out in this,' said Osric.

'No excuse for a lack of vigilance,' said Brusc. 'There, a guard post.'

Two hexagonal bunkers guarded a roadway into the camp that stopped approximately spitting distance from the gateway, already buried by the desert. The gate was a section of chainlink fencing in a wheeled frame, less a defence and more a formality. Osric grunted at the sight of it. 'That'll keep the orks out,' he said dismissively.

The troopers manning the bunker recognised the brothers for what they were and did not present their arms. One came out. Huddled against the wind he seemed tiny and frail, his outline partly hidden by veils of ash so that it looked like he was being abraded to nothing and would be carried off in fragments by the next gust.

The Adeptus Astartes were solid in the teeth of the wind, but the guardsman did not have their strength or their armour, and rocked unsteadily in the eddies whirling off the hospital's units. The man snapped a salute as best he could, a curious version of the aquila, repeated three times over groin, heart and forehead. The brothers banged their arms together in the mark of the Templars' cross in response.

'Lieutenant Sanjeed Ghaskar of the Jopal indentured squadrons,' he shouted over the storm. A turban clad his head, a continuation of it, a band of cloth, looped around his neck and wrapped about his face tight up against his goggled eyes. It didn't quite cover his cheeks and revealed a hint of a glossy black beard. His obeisance paid, he shielded this exposed part of himself with a gloved hand, and hunched over again, his other arm protectively over his stomach. 'We are glad to see you! Or perhaps not,' he yelled. 'The coming of the Angels of Death often presages disaster.'

'We go only where disaster is, this is true,' said Brusc, his voice now projected from his speaker grille at maximum volume. 'It will come here soon enough, I am sure, but not today. We are passing through. There are orders to investigate all Imperial outposts to ensure they have received the command to fall back.'

Ghaskar looked up sharply at that.

'You have not heard? The fall of Acheron?' asked Osric, who now did have to shout. 'It is good that we give you the courtesy of our visit then, as we are not beholden to act on these orders.'

'We had best talk inside. I grant you my permission to enter the Hospice of the Blessed Lady Santanna,' said Ghaskar. He performed a shallow bow.

'Most gracious,' said Osric, somewhat sarcastically. Ghaskar beckoned them on, and the three of them passed through the gate.

Privately Osric added to Brusc, 'It is going to take me a week to repair the finish on my armour.'

'One must honour one's battlegear, did I teach you nothing?' asked Brusc, although his tone was light. This was the way between them – once master and pupil, they had long been friends. Both shared certain characteristics of irreverence. The bond between had always been strong.

'I enjoy it repairing my gear, and I humbly honour it. Who doesn't? It is a fine time to meditate and pay thanks to the Emperor that one still lives and reflect upon the fight. Only it is unsatisfying repairing damage from the weather rather than that won in good, honest battle. What prayer and glory can I offer to the Lord of Man through polishing out sand scratches?'

Brusc looked around as they passed through the rough streets of the facility. It was built on the standard Astra Militarum grid pattern, a north-south and east-west road leading to gate sites, although they had instated only one here, at the west. Side roads led off between buildings. It was small, an unimpressive place barely two hundred metres across each side. A difficult site to hold. A challenge.

'Something tells me brother,' he said, 'that you may soon get your wish to offer true praise. I feel the Emperor's hand at work here.'

They were directed into a long low prefabricatum, one of forty indistinguishable from the rest. Inside was a medicae ward of thirty or so beds. The astonished wounded stared at the giants in their midst as they strode through the flimsy building, showering dust from their scored black armour. The whole prefabricatum rocked under their tread.

Lieutenant Ghaskar led them to a busy woman by a dying man's bed at the far end of the room. 'Sister Rosa of the Hospitallers of the Adepta Sororitas,' he said, then made his leave.

Sister Rosa was a squat woman with hard features and grey hair. Her face was blemished with numerous rad-moles. Her pleasure at seeing fellow warriors of the faith was at best guarded, turning soon to outright annoyance when they relayed their message. She stepped away from the dying man, drawing the Space Marines after her as she checked the charts of other soldiers.

'We cannot leave,' she said.

'You must,' said Brusc. 'This entire sector is collapsing, thanks to the treachery of von Strab. The orks are regrouping, their warbands joining. Their outriders are heading this way.'

'We will remain,' she said stubbornly, 'until the tempest has expended its strength.' She moved onto another bed.

'Sister, this storm will not blow over for several days,' said Brusc.

'And when it does blow over, we shall be ready to depart for Infernus.'

'You must leave now. All forces are falling back to Hive Helsreach. When the storm blows over, the orks will be ready to attack. They will destroy you,' said Brusc sharply.

'Come now, show some respect, she is of a holy order,' said Osric privately. 'She is as marred as you by her service. You do little honour to our order or your title as Sword

Brother.' Publicly, he said, 'Forgive my brother. We are a choleric breed, more given to attack than consideration.'

Sister Rosa pressed her lips tightly together.

'Nevertheless,' Brusc continued, with a glance at his ex-pupil, 'I am correct. We have orders to fall back ourselves. This is no easy thing for us to do. Every part of our being urges us to go onwards and avenge our losses. But we will not. Considered retreat is the right course of action, if only so we might advance again refreshed and rearmed. You must come with us. This hospice was behind friendly lines. It is no longer. The orks are closing in, and will move on you when the weather allows. The materiel is unimportant. Leave now.'

She withdrew her head, sharply, multiplying her chins to three. Her face was etched with a scowl. 'You do not understand. I do not speak of materiel, but the wounded. Not all of my patients can be moved without great care. I cannot pack up the facility at such short notice. I will not go.'

'Then you must bring what you can, and help those who can move. This is no time to be sentimental. We shall offer the Emperor's Mercy to those who will not survive the trip,' said Brusc.

'I have received no orders from my superiors,' she said.

'You have heard them from me,' said Brusc.

'Neither you, brother, nor your Marshal have any right to order me,' she said. '"From many pillars is the Imperium forged, each to its own burden."' she quoted. 'I, like you, am not subject to the whims of the Astra Militarum either. We sisters answer to a higher authority.'

'True,' said Brusc. 'But the orders make sense. Our Marshal has followed suit, ordering us in the same manner that other units have been ordered. He is a wise man, well-versed in the arts of war. His wisdom should be enough to convince you. I question your own wisdom if it is not.'

'What do you suggest then?' huffed Rosa.

'We can offer you our protection and guidance back to Imperial lines. Stay here, and you will perish.'

'If it is the Emperor's will, then so be it,' she said.

'She's a stubborn one,' said Osric privately. 'I like her. She's an awful lot like you.'

The sister stood tall, and continued. 'You are correct. Without you we shall perish. So then do your duty. Remain here and protect us while we make ready to leave,' she said.

Osric gave a throaty chuckle. 'She is like you.'

Brusc shifted his weight, his dust-clogged armour plates rasping over one another under his dirty white surcoat. 'Give me one reason, one reason alone why I should defy the orders of my marshal and stay here to defend this collection of broken men,' he said.

'Blood,' she said immediately. 'Only the blood of the faithful can hold back the darkness. We are all the Emperor's proxies. His light shows the way, but he cannot act directly. Through us,' she pointed at her own chest. 'Through me, him, them, the ill and the wounded. They are all the Emperor's instruments, as much as you are, lesser though they are, broken though they are. They are the blades of His will, they have been tested in battle, and come back honed. When they are healed they will fight better for it, and you would waste them without a thought. You stand there before me, "brother",' she mocked him with the word, 'and chide me for sentimentality, but you are mistaken. It is not sentimentality that will have me stay here, but the Emperor's purpose. I know of your chapter, brother. You crusade and crusade and crusade. But you cannot cleanse the galaxy on your own. Even if you could, could you hold your conquests? Every world? To your credit, your order alone in all the Adeptus Astartes I have witnessed count yourself as true believers, warriors of the Divine Emperor. So tell me, crusader, by whose authority do you cast aside the instruments of our God? You discard His tools, and in doing so you defy His will. Not even your vaunted marshal has the impertinence for that.'

Brusc stared at the woman. Her head came only as high as the heraldic cross on his surcoat. He considered leaving, he considered telling her that, actually, it was by Marshal Ricard's authority that he would abandon these broken tools of the Emperor to the choking sands because there were others more worthy of his efforts.

He did not. Sister Rosa stared unwaveringly at him, her brows drawn in. Her ruined face crinkled around the eyes. Her hand leapt to her chest when Brusc burst into loud laughter.

She recovered her composure with admirable speed. 'Do you mock me? Do you mock my words? Do you mock the Emperor?'

'No, no!' said Brusc. 'It is a long time since I have been upbraided so by a mortal. You remind me of someone I knew a long time ago.'

'You ignored her too, I suppose? Go then,' she said. 'Leave us here to die. Let your own laughter and shame hound you across the wastes.'

Brusc laid a massive hand on her shoulder, his gauntlet

engulfing it entirely. He kneeled in front of her and bowed his head, his mirth gone.

'I have my reason, holy sister,' he said. 'You speak well. I am shamed.' He looked up at her, and carefully removed his helmet, setting it to the side on the floor. His burned skull – covered in smooth synthetic skin and blotched scar tissue, his scalp patched unevenly with hair – held no horror for her, and she saw the humour had not entirely left his face, although it was leavened now with the utmost sincerity.

'The Black Templars will fight by your side,' he said.

She nodded her thanks. 'Your Reclusiarch Grimaldus has won a great victory at Helsreach. I hear he clawed his way from the rubble of the Temple of the Emperor Ascendant. If your faith is as true as you say, then you must see the hand of the Emperor in this. He watches over us all. His attention is on this world. If we are true to our purpose and loud in our prayers then we will prevail. I will ensure all that can be done to speed the evacuation, is done.'

'We will pray for your efforts, and freely offer any assistance you might deem necessary.'

She curtly nodded once and bustled off, giving orders as she went. Activity burst around her like shrapnel from a bomb.

Osric watched her go. 'See, I knew I liked her,' he said.

'Brother Osric, do not speak to me like that again, the way you did in front of Sister Rosa.'

'I was right to do so, brother,' said Osric amiably. 'You were being unreasonable.'

'Yes,' said Brusc. 'Yes, you were, and yes, I was. Diplomacy is not my strongest attribute. Still, do not do it again.'

Osric made a little, dismissive noise. 'Then do not give me cause to. You are our leader here, brother – we expect the best of you. If you're not going to live up to the example required then I reserve the right to remind you.'

Brusc laughed – he was ever a man quick to anger and quick to laughter. Brother Osric rather relied on that, he always had. 'You should be a Sword Brother, not me.'

'Maybe,' said Osric. He paused, then spoke in earnest. 'Recommend me, brother, enter my name into the ring of honour. My sword is ready for the challenge.'

'Seriously?' asked Brusc. 'You want me to put you forward? You might find yourself duelling with me for your place. We both know who the better swordsman is.'

Osric nodded. 'Nevertheless, I am deadly serious. I am ready.'

Brusc retrieved his helmet, covered his mutilated face and walked out from the ward. 'I'll consider it. Emperor alone knows too many of our best have fallen here. But before you face the blades of the Sword Brethren, we must survive the attentions of the foe.'

Seven hours later, when preparations to abandon the hospice were well underway, the storm lifted. Armageddon's sun peered meekly through the whirling screens of dust and ash spat out by the world's volcanoes. It was so wan that Brusc could look it full on without filtering. It had become a pale smear, the light it shone on the Ash Wastes anaemic. He and the others walked the perimeter. The indentured men of Jopal needed no overseeing, but the presence of the Angels of Death inspired and frightened them in equal measure, and they worked all the harder when they paced by. Ghaskar's small garrison had turned out in full, bolstered by many of the less gravely sick. Barricades were being erected on every street. Fire positions covered the major intersections. Heavy weapons batteries were arrayed to provide linked fields of fire. Men hurried to and fro, stocking the line with crates of spare ammunition and water butts.

'By the Throne,' said Osric as he surveyed the featureless landscape beyond the defence line, 'what a miserable place to die.'

Brusc gave him a look, one Osric could feel even though Brusc wore his helmet. Despite Brusc's intentions, it made Osric smile.

'And we should not die, when so many others have?' said Brusc.

'Emperor willing, no,' said Osric. He spat ashy sand from his mouth with an irritated expression. The air was thick with it still and he had unwisely removed his helmet. 'Death is our ultimate reward, but I am not yet ready for it. My crusading days are far from done. I have much blood to spill for the Emperor yet. If he decrees I am to die here, then that is His will and I accept it, but…' his voice trailed off. 'Still, visibility's back up to several hundred metres,' said Osric. 'We'll be able to select targets at maximum range. I hate firing blind.'

'The way you fire, I doubt it would matter.'

'Blade work's more my forte, I admit,' Osric said. 'You should have trained me better.'

'Defence in depth – these Jopali are impressive,' said Sunno. 'What forces do we have?'

'Two hundred and fifty-three healthy men, almost that again walking wounded. Seven Hospitaller Warrior-Medicae, twenty-six medical servitors. Fifteen pieces of light ordinance, not counting those mounted the external bunkers. Four Chimeras, a Taurox, our own *Cataphraxes*, us and a preacher.'

'Not the greatest army on Armageddon,' said Sunno. 'Will it be enough?'

'We had better hope so,' said Brusc. He clapped Sunno on the pauldron. 'But I have fought worse odds.'

'I have met some ferocious preachers in my time,' said Sunno.

'Brother Osric is right, of course...' said Brusc.

'When am I not?'

'...the Jopal Indentured will need every advantage. The further they can fire, and the less atmospheric dissipation to their weapons, the better.' Brusc eyed a trooper's lasgun disdainfully. 'They would be better served by other guns.'

'That is all they have,' said Sunno grimly.

'Then they will have to do, as they have done on a million battlefields across the galaxy since the Emperor took his crusade to the stars.'

'Listen to him, novitiates!' said Osric, turning to face the two squires trailing them. He gestured expansively. 'He speaks well, it is not our right to dismiss any servant of the Emperor. For He has ordained that we fight together on this battlefield! It is his will that brings us here, just as it is His will that we are made to protect the likes of these unaltered men. Too many of the Adeptus Astartes allow their superiority to turn to contempt for the Emperor's subjects. Never forget what we were made for, and that valour can be contained in the most fragile of vessels. Service can be rendered by all.'

'Praise be,' said Sunno and Brusc.

The Guardsmen stood taller at mention of their valour. Doneal and Marcomar nodded solemnly. Osric let them pass him then slapped them on the back, staggering them. 'Be of better cheer, lads, for soon we fight the ork!'

'I would have vengeance,' said Marcomar quietly.

'And you shall have it novitiate, fear not,' said Sunno.

Brusc brought his small squad to a stop. 'Now, Brother Marcomar, up on that roof with your sniper rifle.' Brusc pointed to the highest roof in the battered facility, a delta-level comms tower, its dishes and antennae useless. 'Tell me, when the battle is upon us, what do you aim for?'

Marcomar's response was leaden but quick. 'Aim for the largest, their officer cadre and specialists. Track and eliminate threats. Destroy those that would threaten the weakest points of our line.' His eyes slid slowly to his left, toward the Guardsmen dragging open crates of lasgun packs to the defence line.

Osric cleared his throat, a slight shake of his head. 'Remember what I just said, neophyte.' Marcomar nodded his understanding and stared ahead.

'Go on then,' said Brusc. 'To your station.'

Marcomar nodded, shifting his grip on his gun bag, and went to his post.

Sister Rosa was passing and stopped at Brusc's shoulder. She made little concession to the harsh environment beyond a snug rebreather, an apron and protective sleeves over her robes. Brusc suspected that was more to protect them, not her.

'Your preparations go well? My sisters and laity are ready to aid the wounded. For now they pack apace.'

'As well as can be hoped, sister,' said Brusc. 'We have little to do. Your Lieutenant Ghaskar is a capable man.' He looked her up and down. 'Do you not have something... Do you not have more appropriate attire for war?'

She shook his concerns away with one hand, the other clutched rolls of bandages tight to her chest. 'I have performed my duty as warrior-medicae to both the Astra Militarum and Sisters of Battle, brother,' she said. 'But my armour no longer fits, and my fighting days are long behind me. The Emperor's grace is enough protection for me.' She rapped on his chest with a knuckle. 'Not all the faithful have need of such unsubtle shields.'

Brusc ignored her jibe. 'And how are the preparations?'

She pointed away to the square at the centre of the compound where men loaded seven massive haulers standing nose to tail in a circle. The Space Marine's Rhino waited silently at the entrance to the road leading to the gate, a dog guarding a herd of kine.

'We are nearly done. We shall have to abandon the structure, of course, but I have loaded all movable supplies and equipment. Those wounded that cannot fight are ready to be put onboard. The most critical cases we shall leave until last, but they are prepared.'

'Be ready. If we beat this attack back, we shall need to depart immediately, because orks will come quickly to any rumour of battle. Do you understand?'

'I understand.' She followed Brusc's gaze, her eyes lighting on Marcomar as he made himself ready. He carefully removed his weapon's dust cover, and was beginning the rituals of preparation.

'You have other things on your mind, I see,' she said, the gentlest words she had spoken to Brusc.

'His master fell six days ago. We were on long range patrol for our crusade before we were recalled, and were ambushed. We slaughtered them all, but I lost two brothers, adding to three already fallen. It is hard on the novitiates, when their knight is slain,' said Brusc quietly. 'But he has taken it especially badly, and it will go against him. There is no room for fear or shock in the Adeptus Astartes. Marcomar's failure will be a further loss that will be difficult to bear.'

'Is he certain to fail? I have seen the meekest sister made a tigress in battle, brother, but it takes time. Will another take on his training?'

Brusc shrugged, a mighty movement that set his pauldrons shifting like troubled mountains. 'It is not a certainty, we see it as a personal failing to allow our knight to fall. There is little the novitiate can do to protect their masters in most cases – they are not full brothers after all – but even so, some of the initiates regard it as a stain on the squire's honour if they do not perish with their knight, even though they should know better.' He regarded the morose novitiate, appraising his actions. 'And there will be plenty of masterless boys come the end of this war, that is certain.'

He looked out at the desert. Sister Rosa started to speak, but Brusc raised a hand, silencing her. His helmet lenses whirred as they focused on something beyond the reach of human sight.

'Dust plumes,' he said. 'They are coming. They are coming!' he shouted, his voice blaring from his vox-grille. 'Stand ready!'

THE ORKS CAME at them as the sun entered the last quarter of the day. A solid wall of flesh marching over the wastes, their bright totems were caked in dust, whatever boasts they proclaimed lost beneath Armageddon's grey coat. In the dun light of late afternoon they appeared as an army of ghosts out of the haze, fanged and terrible. Their chanting was a throbbing roar. Already the crackle and pop of weapons fire rang out. Too far away to hit the defenders of the hospital, they fired into the air from excitement. A handful of light buggies and bikes rushed ceaselessly back and forth in front of the horde, throwing up plumes of ash.

'Well,' said Osric. 'No tanks. That's something. At least you won't miss, novitiates.' He had replaced his helmet on his head, and spoke to both neophytes through the vox. Marcomar aside, the Black Templars stood together: Sunno, Brusc, Osric and Doneal. All had their weapons in hand – bolt pistol and chainsword for the initiates, while Doneal carried a pistol the same as his masters, but in his off hand he held a great combat knife the length of a man's thighbone.

'Nor will you, Osric,' said Brusc. 'Don't listen to him, he's the worst shot in the crusade.'

'You do know, young one, that Sword Brother Brusc here was my knight and I his squire? The pupil learns as much as he can from the master,' said Osric. 'In the matter of marksmanship, I learned only as much as I could.'

'Truly?' asked Doneal.

'You seem surprised, boy, but we all have been what you are now. Besides, it was a long time ago, when our leader here had a prettier face.'

'War demands not beauty, but slaughter,' said Brusc.

'Ah, but there is art in war. Art indeed. Any art is beautiful, especially that of death.'

'Praise be, brother,' said Sunno.

'We shall pray,' Brusc said, without preamble. Together, the Space Marines knelt in the dust, crossing their arms and weapons over their chests, bowing their heads. Marcomar followed suit on the platform of the comms tower.

'Lead us, brother,' said Osric. No trace of levity was in his voice.

When Brusc spoke next, he did so loudly and clearly through his helmet vox. The men on the defence line looked back over their shoulders away from the foe. They ceased to finger their weapons so nervously. Many of them dropped their heads, and muttered prayers of their own; the rites of the Adeptus Astartes were strange to them.

'Emperor! Lord of all Mankind, he who came among the weakling children of Terra and stood against the terrors of an uncaring universe. Emperor! We, the sons of Your son, gene-forged to Your design, kneel here in the dust of this far-flung world, far from Your throne. Emperor! We ask not for Your mercy, or for Your protection. We do not ask for Your favour save this: that we fight with all the strength You saw fit to bestow upon us, and in doing so further the victory of Your most holy war, the crusade that never ends. Guide our arms, guide our aim, see that we make good count of the foe so that fewer horrors might assail mankind, Your servants, and stand in the way of Your mastery of the stars! We five, few that we are, so make this oath: That we shall not falter.'

'That we shall not falter,' repeated the others.

'That we shall not fail.'

'That we shall not fail,' the response came.

'That we shall not bring dishonour unto you.'

'No dishonour! This we swear!' they all shouted.

Brusc rose to his feet. He held aloft his chainsword

and turned on the spot, showing the weapon to everyone around him. The wind, reduced to little more than a hot breath, stirred his dirty surcoat and the fresh oath papers attached to his armour. 'No pity! No remorse! No fear!' he roared.

This time, the response issued from everyone within the compound.

He nodded to his followers. They stood.

'It is time we were about our business,' he said.

The rattle of chains oath-chains being attached to sword hilt and pistol butt was the Black Templars' response.

A hundred metres away to the left, on the far side of the compound, heavy bolters chattered. Explosions rumbled as the ork outriders were caught.

Osric raised his bolt pistol and took aim. The orks were a way off yet, well out of range of his pistol, yet he picked a target, locked his arm, held it steady and waited.

It was an inevitability that the orks would come over the line. They were many, and the men of Jopal of insufficient numbers to keep them back by weight of fire alone.

Nevertheless, many greenskins fell, burned by lasfire before the orks breached the walls. They came through in three places more or less simultaneously. The indentured men of Jopal reeled from this assault, shocked by the orks' brutality and their cunningly coordinated attack.

Brusc found little new. He had fought the orks many times. There were not the unthinking brutes propaganda would have the men of the Astra Militarum believe. He and his brothers separated and went to the breaches, engaging the orks hand to hand. Relieved, the lesser men fell back to barricades in the streets. For a time, Brusc fought alone. Orks roared and hurled themselves at him. The power of their blows rocked him on his feet, but he found tranquillity there in the heat of the melee, and he attained a higher level of intimacy with the Lord of Man through these most holy rites of battle.

He dispatched an opponent with a backwards thrust through the neck. The ork's head juddered as his chainsword's teeth ground their way through its spine. A twisting jerk freed the blade from the neck. The ork's head came with it. The body collapsed to its knees, fountaining dark red blood all over Brusc. Then the Jopali had their position and new firing solutions. They opened up, felling the last of the orks at Brusc's breach. He searched for new targets, but found none.

Brusc barely had time to draw breath when a desperate cry went up over the vox, a signifier in Brusc's helm indicating it came from one of the human officers. If it was Ghaskar, he could not tell for its panicked thickness.

'Keep them away from the transports! Keep them away!'

He turned his back on the defence wall, where the next wave of screaming xenos savages was being gunned down by disciplined lasfire, and looked to the centre of the compound.

Half a dozen leader-orks had forced their way to the very heart of the hospital; giants clad in hissing suits of armour. Fifteen, perhaps more, of the lesser kind loped alongside them, their huge rifles spitting fire. In the midst of them all went one even greater, a mighty ork-king, half Brusc's height again. Bright yellow patterned with black showed through the dust and ash caking its suit. The armour encased it almost completely, covering its head, its eyes protected by thick lenses of green glass and the jaw hidden behind a serrated metal bevoir cast in the shape of a jaw. Only the joints were their weakness. Brusc's heart soared at the sight of it.

'Here is a foe! Here is honour! Black Templars, to me!'

Without waiting for his men, Brusc ran down the avenue toward the leader orks as they advanced on the trucks. The orks did not fire upon the vehicles, slaughtering only the men. Providence was with humanity – plunder was the orks' intent. As orks approached the silent *Cataphraxes*, the black knights of Dorn crashed into the guard with a noise like thunder. Coming from three directions, they barged their way through the lesser creatures by dint of strength alone, crushing and slashing them down. Their bolt pistols sang the clamorous hymns of death until their ammunition was spent and the weapons were dropped to swing by their lanyards, trailing smoke like censers from glowing barrels.

This was prayer for the Black Templars. War was their worship, the battlefield their temple. Hymns ringing from their vox-grilles, they gripped their chainswords two handed and hewed at the foe. Sunno accounted for two of the guard creatures, ducking below their ponderously swinging arms to despatch them one after the other with artful blows – the first to the neck, the second gutted and beheaded as it fell forward. The snap of Marcomar's sniper rifle was the call of retribution upon the wind – pure and clean it cut through the brutish barks of orkish gunfire, felling one after another of the lighter armoured creatures. Brusc found himself duelling with a pair of giants. Both his hearts pumped hard, flooding his system with the blessings of the Emperor. Time slowed, and he sang the Hymn of Hate to the beat of his blows.

Soon the majority of the orks lay dead, leaking blood and machine fluids into the greedy ash. Over their slumped forms Brusc caught sight of Osric. Alone he had gone to fight with the ork-king. Alone, he had fallen into peril. The ork had Osric in one massive claw, the scissor blades crushing the armour of his forearm. Osric dangled, his battleplate breached in three places. He swung his legs in fruitless kicks at the ork, his curses loud in Brusc's ear pieces.

The teeth-track of Brusc's sword was clogged with tough ork flesh. The motor whined dangerously, smoke issuing from its exhaust. He released its trigger before it burned out, unclipped its lanyard and flung the weapon aside with a prayer of apology. As he ran to Osric's aid he slammed home a fresh magazine into his bolt pistol. By the time he had snatched his combat blade from its sheath, his armour-aided legs were pushing him speedily at the king.

Osric gave up trying to free his arm and reached for a grenade. Brusc launched himself through the air, smashing into the scrap armour of the ork-king. The plangence of their meeting was the voice of a bell in some temple of belligerence. The ork staggered. With surprising speed it swung round, hurling Osric at Brusc's head. The Sword Brother ducked, firing as he did. Osric hit a prefab's wall, crumpling it and streaking it with his blood as he fell to the ground. Brusc's bolts sparked off the ork-king's armour or exploded without effect on the surface. One found an unprotected spot. When it blew, gobbets of flesh rained outwards, but the ork was not slowed. Whatever pain it felt only served to stoke its fury, and it came at Brusc fast, the crude pistons on its warsuit hissing gas.

Brusc dodged a blow, the ork's giant shears clanging shut

inches from his helm's muzzle. He riposted with his knife, driving it at the ork's forearm, seeking the gap at the elbow where dirty green skin was visible. The ork was too agile, the knife hit the armour. The plating on the lord shamed a tank. Brusc's thrust gouged a bright silver streak in the metal, peeling away a long curl of swarf, but no more than that. The ork backhanded him, swinging its claw-clad fist into his chest. Brusc flew backwards, alarm signals peeping in his helmet as he crashed to the floor. His visor display jumped, the static of it conspiring with the blood running down over his lenses to limit his vision. The ork was on him again, reaching for him. Then it had him, one shear about his neck, the other around his thighs. Roaring its triumph, the ork-king lofted him upwards, holding its trophy over its head for all his slaves to see.

'Forgive me, Emperor, when we meet,' shouted Brusc, 'for I have spilled too little blood in your name.'

The expected pressure, the crushing of metal and flesh, never came. The ork-king had stopped in his tracks. Brusc twisted around in its grasp, his battleplate squealing against the claw's razored edges.

The ork's face was still twisted in triumph, the great bucket jaw of the armour swung open to roar, but behind the metal his tongue lolled from his teeth. A twist of white smoke rose coyly from its open mouth, the only sign of the sniper shot that had slain it. Its armour held its corpse in position. It toppled slowly over backwards with Brusc still trapped in its claws.

'Forgive me, my lord,' said Marcomar over the vox. 'I had to wait until opportunity presented itself.'

There was a steeliness in his voice that had been lacking before.

'Then you have had your vengeance, novitiate,' said Brusc.

'Indeed. Praise be.'

In that moment, Brusc knew Marcomar would not fail after all.

By the time he had extricated himself from the dead warlord's grasp, the orks were in flight. Their king slain and his cohorts fallen, the lesser orks broke and ran, leaving many of their dead upon the field. Bright laser light and heavy bolter shells slew more as the fled, the surviving men of Jopal jeering at their rout. The Black Templars stayed with the haulers. Sunno and Doneal worked in tandem, despatching stragglers and wounded xenos. Doneal was savage and skilled. He would make a fine battle-brother.

Only when he was sure that the battle was finished did Brusc go to Osric's side.

Osric lay with his legs out. He had managed to haul himself into a sitting position, so that his powerplant rested on the wall, but had got no further. The gashes in his armour sparked. Red meat was revealed beneath.

'That was foolish, brother.' Brusc switched his flickering helm display around, bringing up the vital signs of his ex-pupil and friend as he knelt at the younger Space Marine's side. Both heartbeats were weak, and growing weaker. Osric's armour was flooding his body with drugs from its pharmacopeia, but his wounds were deep and neither medicament nor his body's innate gifts could stem the tide of blood. Bright crimson poured from the rents in Osric's plate, staining the ground around him; far too much of it.

'I was trying to impress you, brother,' said Osric. He

attempted a laugh, but it gurgled horribly and became a bubbling cough. It took a moment for him to recover. 'Perhaps if I had taken his head,' he gasped, 'then you would not have hesitated to present me in the Circle of Honour.'

'Perhaps,' said Brusc. 'But his death bought honour for Marcomar instead.'

'All is not lost then,' said Osric. 'You must give him further chance. I would take him to squire myself, if I do not die.'

'Lie still, do not speak. You have been grievously wounded.' Brusc spoke softly. He rested his hand on Osric's helm, an echo of a parent touching the brow of a sick child. The brothers were all the family any of them would ever know, the only blood.

Osric raised a wavering hand and gripped Brusc's forearm. 'I fought well, do not deny me that.'

'You fought well, my friend.'

Brusc stood, and Osric's enfeebled hand skidded from his battleplate to lie curled on the stained earth. His head lolled. Orderlies and sisters from Sister Rosa's station were running to the fallen Space Marine. They openly wept to see an angel of their god thusly cast down.

Sister Rosa was with them, bloodied, but still whole. 'We shall do what we can for him, brother,' she said.

Brusc shrugged as if it mattered not if they did or did not, although it mattered to him a great deal. He pointed at the spreading pool beneath Osric. The sand was saturated. 'Witness, sister! It is as you said – there is only blood. We all bleed it, mighty and meek, high and lowly. The blood of the faithful waters the earth of every Imperial world, as is only right. Remember him. Remember the blood he has shed for you.'

The orderlies struggled to move Osric's armoured body onto a stretcher that was far too short for his height. Brusc watched dispassionately. Losing patience with them, Rosa snapped and sent for medical servitors. 'Quickly now! He is dying!'

In Brusc's helmet, Osric's vital signs became erratic. It would not be long now.

'Do not leave his body. He has one more service to render.'

'Yes, brother,' said Sister Rosa.

He stared down at his dying brother. 'See that you are ready to depart, sister. The orks will return. We leave in ten minutes.'

Without looking back, he strode toward *Cataphraxes*.

SEASON
OF SHADOWS

THE SEASON OF Fire abated. The last plumes of ash coughed from Armageddon's volcanoes. Dying winds hurried the season's final storms to stillness. Searing heat gave way as the world was plunged into a short, volcanic winter. At Armageddon's poles, dirty snow fell.

The Season of Shadows had begun.

In peaceful times this cessation of the storms was a respite for men. The season was well named, for the land was dark and cool. It was a time for quiet doings, although thunderous industry never ceased. This year was different; the choking ash would be missed. As soon as the skies began to clear, the fires of war rekindled. Orks came out from their hiding places and marched upon the hives of Armageddon once more.

'Another charge brother! Quickly!'

In a twilight-noon born of ash the shrouded sun smouldered upon a field-hospital, recently attacked and soon to be abandoned. Within its broken confines Black Templars Space Marines worked with haste.

Sword Brother Brusc, the leader of this much depleted reconnaissance group not long on Armageddon, tossed a bulky demo pack at Brother Sunno as easily as a normal man might throw an egg. Sunno grabbed it from the air and slapped it onto the leg of the comms tower. Made redundant by the shattering of the world's data network, the tower was to be felled just the same, as insisted upon by Adeptus Astartes thoroughness.

A fitful wind moaned through tension cables, wrapping short-lived veils of dust around support struts. Brusc glanced skyward. The sun was a round circle, a hole punched in dark cloth. Brighter than in the storms of the previous day, still it could be stared at with unshielded eyes.

Sunno's neophyte, Doneal, signalled from a roof on the other side of the compound, hand in the air and forefinger describing a circle.

'That's the last, brother,' Sunno said, dragging Brusc's attention from the dark skies. 'Doneal and Marcomar are done.'

'Good. We shall leave nothing for the orks,' said Brusc, his voice projecting from his helmet's vox-grille.

'To *Cataphraxes* then,' said Sunno.

'Immediately. Neophytes, rejoin us.'

'Yes, my lord,' the two young Space Marines said in unison.

The field hospital heaved with activity. Ork corpses from the recent assault lay along every road. Dying men screamed. Shouting squads of Jopal Indentured hurried about, stripping equipment from the prefabricatums and the dead, moving debris from the evacuation's path. Machine noise roared high periodically, drowning out the voices of men. Earth movers grumbled, shunting aside squealing piles of metal. In the marshalling yard, tanks puttered as their drivers ran engines gently to clear them of dust.

This lone subgroup of the Black Templars Ash Wastes Crusade gathered before their Rhino, *Cataphraxes*.

'How long until they come, my lords?' asked Doneal.

'Not long, boy,' said Sunno. 'Not long.'

'At least the clear skies are holding.'

Brusc shot the boy a dark look. Ordinarily light of spirit, Brusc was not currently disposed to optimism. 'The Season of Shadows is yet to begin in earnest. It might not last,' he said. He looked up again, searching for something the others could not see. 'In truth we are at the mercy of the weather, whatever it does.'

Doneal wordlessly asked for clarification.

'Ash storms might mask us as easily as they could kill us, neophyte,' said Sunno. 'When our dust plumes go skyward, the orks can see us from miles away.'

Brusc acknowledged Sunno's statement with a noise in his throat.

The Black Templars Rhino *Cataphraxes* waited at the mouth of the complex's central square, black armour rubbed down to its undercoat by the fury of Armageddon's abrasive winds. A pintle-mounted storm bolter topped its front.

Inside his blank-faced Crusader helm, Sunno smiled. '*Cataphraxes*'s engine is cold, but he is ready, brother. Can you feel his anticipation?'

'I cannot,' said Brusc. 'I do not share your affinity for the machine's soul.'

'Such a shame, brother. His is a holy soul, vengeful. He hears news of Osric's fall and wishes to avenge his brother.'

Osric had fallen in battle with the orks. He had been Brusc's last neophyte before he won through to the Sword Brethren. He had been Brusc's friend.

Seven large haulers were behind the tank, nose to tail in a convoy line wrapped round all sides of the hospital's central square. Double-decker tractor units provided motive power. Their armoured cabs were equipped with stacked pairs of ball-mounted heavy stubbers. Each tractor unit was motivated by six double tyres as tall as men. Massive, articulated trailers already loaded with a container apiece waited behind them. These were built to the same basic standard template construct pattern as the prefabricatums. Had they time to properly dismantle the hospital then the wards would have been stacked atop the containers, fitting together like child's construction bricks, but there was no time, and the hospital was to be destroyed.

Medicae orderlies and sisters hospitaller were coming out of the emptying wards, carrying the last, most seriously wounded patients aboard. Brusc wondered which truck carried Osric's body.

'Brother Sunno, go to *Cataphraxes*,' he ordered. 'Neophyte Doneal, you are to remain with your master. Man *Cataphraxes*'s armament. Keep your eyes sharp.'

'Yes, my lord.'

'Neophyte Marcomar, you have no master. Until you are chosen again you will remain with me.'

The neophyte fell in behind him silently. He had lost his own knight several days before the squad had come upon the hospital, and remained withdrawn.

'You have replaced your rifle's dust cover,' Brusc said approvingly.

'Yes, my lord.'

'Good. A warrior should guard his wargear with his life. Honour your weapons the way you honour the Emperor, and both will shield you.'

'Yes, my lord.'

They went to the administration building, a prefabricatum identical to all the others, marked out only by the wind-scoured image of a cracked chalice emblazoned upon the side.

The doors to the unit were open. Sister Rosa, administratrix of the hospital, directed her staff. She was framed in the building's interior light, bright in the grim noon.

'We are ready,' said Brusc.

'As are we,' said Sister Rosa. Her rad-marked face was harried, features drawn with stress and lack of sleep. 'There are seven we cannot move. They will suffer if we try.'

'Do you wish us to administer mercy?'

'We do not need you to perform our duties for us, brother. My sisters do so now.'

'Do they die well?'

'They do, brother,' said Sister Rosa.

Brusc shifted, looked over his shoulder at the men and women striving to get everything done. 'That is good,' he said eventually. 'Record their names and we will honour them in our prayers. They do not die in battle, but their sacrifice is no less noble.'

An Imperial Guard officer came into the square, five squads jogging behind him with purpose. He halted and his men formed up behind him. Not one of the squads was at full strength. Most of the soldiers bore minor wounds. All of them were tired. They stood tall nonetheless.

'Lieutenant Ghaskar,' said Brusc.

Ghaskar bowed. 'My lord. We are prepared. All we wait for is your word.'

'Then you have it,' said Brusc.

Ghaskar yelled orders in his odd Gothic dialect. His men broke from attention, some running for the tractor cabs, the rest running for ladders attached to the sides of the trailers.

Around the top of each container was a low rail, part of the locking mechanism of the stacking system, scant protection for the Jopali. The men jammed themselves against these, lying flat, guns pointing out all round. The wiser ones lashed ropes around their ankles and rails then urged the less experienced to do the same.

'Sister Rosa,' said Brusc. 'We shall ride the lead hauler. My brothers will watch from the front. We will do all we can to ensure that as many as possible can survive.'

'I will be praying for us all,' she said.

Brusc marched back to the Rhino. The men atop the trucks nodded at him, warrior to warrior, or worshipfully made the Jopali's triple version of the aquila, each according to his temperament.

'Wait here,' he said to Marcomar.

As Brusc walked up the ramp into the Rhino, Sunno spoke to him over his shoulder through the open door of the driver's cab. He had taken his helmet off, a direct line ran from his spinal interface socket into the tank.

'I am in communion with *Cataphraxes*, brother. We pray together.'

'My bolter,' explained Brusc. 'Some range may be

advantageous here.' He retrieved the weapon from the rack at the forward right of the compartment, but did not remove his bloodied chainsword or bolt pistol from his waist, he would need all his holy tools before the day was out. He checked the Rhino's augur suite. 'No sign of them,' said Brusc. 'The Emperor may yet be with us.'

He collected Marcomar and headed for the lead hauler. As he mounted the ladder the men above fell silent. The truck trailer rocked as he climbed. Once on the roof, he took one step to the centre and mag-locked his boots to the metal.

There were six Jopali on top of the truck. Lying at his feet they looked like children. Two of them made obeisance to him, bowing repeatedly and pressing their heads to metal.

'Stop,' said Brusc. 'Do not bow to us.'

'But you are the Angels of Death!' said one. He had his goggles off, exposing a strip of dark skin between his helmet and scarf. His eyes were luminously white in his dirty face.

'We are the instruments of the Emperor. We are not gods. Do not bow to me,' said Brusc gruffly.

Marcomar took up station behind the sword brother, lying as low as his physique and carapace armour would allow. He unwrapped his sniper rifle.

'Brother Sunno, beseech *Cataphraxes* to take us from here,' Brusc voxed.

'Yes, brother.'

A second later *Cataphraxes*'s engine roared into life. The shouting in the camp became frantic. Stragglers scrambled into the side and rear doors of the containers. Six muffled bolt shots sounded from inside the complex. Six Adepta

Sororitas Combat-Medicae, cowled and clad in light power armour, came walking slowly out from the buildings. Their songs of loss were drowned out by igniting engines as one by one the tractor units started up, making a toneless choir of their own. The heavy stink of burning hydrocarbons washed back from their tall exhausts, the kind that, were Brusc's air not filtered by his helmet, would have coated his throat with greasy particulates.

Brusc surveyed the camp. Smoke rose from a couple of burning prefabricatums torched by the greenskins. Orks lay where they had fallen. There were a great many of them. Brusc was impressed by the Jopali's mettle.

The few troopers remaining outside the trucks were throwing down the barricades on the road leading to the gate. Vox chatter between the Jopali increased as roll calls were undertaken. Doors slammed.

Sister Rosa was the last to leave the administratum building. She looked up at Brusc standing upon the roof, her gaze piercing. Both of them were scarred. She by radiation burns gained in the course of their duties, he from battle. Both of them served, in their own way. Brusc acknowledged her with a nod.

'All are aboard,' Ghaskar notified him. 'We may depart when you command, my lord.'

'Then may the Emperor guide us all through storm and foe to safe harbour.' Brusc spoke grimly. His usual humour was absent; he could not think joyous thoughts while Osric lay dead. He closed his eyes and prayed silently.

Emperor, I would gladly have left fifty lesser men here dead, if Osric could have lived. I should not feel this way, but I do. Have mercy on me that I recognise it, though I cannot prevent my feeling it.

A final door slammed. Sister Rosa was reported aboard. 'Brother Sunno, lead us out.'

Cataphraxes gave a satisfied roar and rumbled forward, pushing the remnants of barricades aside, crushing dead orks and dead men alike into pulp underneath its treads.

Brusc lurched as the truck set off. Away to the west side of the camp dust swirled around the Jopali's transports, making their way around the perimeter road to the gate – four Chimeras, a Taurox Prime command tank, and a Salamander Scout, its open compartment covered by a taut tarpaulin.

Sunno drove *Cataphraxes* right through the flimsy gates, chain-link wire on a tube-steel frame. They leapt and quivered under the tank like a dying thing, chinking as the following trucks rode over them.

On the plain before the camp the Chimeras fell in either side of the column. The Taurox fell back, trailing the last truck. Orders crackled from Ghaskar, and the Salamander leapt forward, sending twin tails of dust high into the air.

All around the hospital, ork corpses were black shadows on the ashy sand.

'There is no sign of a single living greenskin,' said Ghaskar.

'I see nothing either,' said Sunno. 'Our escape has gone unnoticed.'

'Remain vigilant,' said Brusc. 'Now we are underway, we are at risk from marauders. There are many operating in this area now that the storms are passing.' He glanced up at the sky. 'I had hoped the storms would return, to mask our passing, but it appears not to be so. The Season of Fire has spent its fury.'

He watched the hospital recede. A detonation rune burned in his visor display.

A difficult choice, he thought. Leave it standing and the greenskins will be enriched. Destroy it, and signal that we are leaving.

The convoy growled up over a low rise, turning to the west to skirt a field of ash dunes. The wind was strong there, sending sheets of dust from the dune's scimitar-ridges.

When they were a couple of kilometres distant and the compound was receding into the haze, Brusc detonated the demolition charges. Fire leapt up from every part of the complex, bursting apart the prefabricatums and lifting their sheeting into the air. They caught the wind, blowing off to the west as if following the convoy. The sounds of the detonation reached Brusc a half second later, a series of puny firecracker pops and rippling metallic crashes.

He watched the field hospital burn until it was lost to the undifferentiated landscapes of the Ash Wastes.

The convoy rumbled onward unopposed. The winds rose and fell, sometimes choking the air with fine ash so that visibility dropped to nothing. The great storms of the Season of Fire were nearly done. The wind dropped, the curtains of ash parting to reveal a parched, dead landscape. Regarding the woeful state of Armageddon, mankind had much to answer for. There were abandoned facilities poking from smooth-sided dunes, expanses of sand garishly stained by industrial by-products, roads that went nowhere and hills cleaved in two – all their worth was burrowed out of them, the hints of giant pits in the ground flooded now with ash. Armageddon had never been a gentle world; its yearly volcanic tantrums were proof of that.

Consequently there were few signs of life of any kind.

Copses of stumpy vennenum marked dust-drowned oases. Thickets of dead men's fingers crowded the leeward slopes of stony hills, as tangled as briars. Sometimes things scuttled within them, but the movements were those of small vermin and rapidly gone.

The signs of war were everywhere they cared to look. Columns of smoke rose on the horizon, and leagues-distant artillery duels rumbled. Contrails streaked the glowering sky. They passed through a field of rusting tank shells, leftovers from the battles of an earlier age. War was all about them yet they were alone.

For a hot day and freezing night the convoy headed west. Twice they stopped so that the Jopali might change shifts, swapping from cab to roof and back again. At night they dozed at their stations. Throughout it all, Brusc and Marcomar maintained an unsleeping vigilance. Only infrequently did he check in with Sunno or Lieutenant Ghaskar.

As a second dawn stained the grey-ash deserts a hostile vermillion, they stopped for a third time. Ghaskar, Brusc and Sunno held a council of war.

'There's a dead valley ahead, brother,' said Sunno. 'Dry river bed, a good natural road. Danger of ambush, though. Topographical data says it runs right down to the Mortis river. Follow that, and we'll be at the Helsreach perimeter in another twenty hours.'

'There are supply convoys and relief columns running up and down the river highway in great numbers,' said Ghaskar. 'We would be safe there, back under the protection of Imperial forces.'

'He's right about that, brother,' said Sunno. 'But we might not survive to get there. The valley's a prime ambush spot. We will have nearly one hundred kilometres to drive before we hit Imperial pickets.'

'Where are the enemy?' asked Brusc. 'Have we had any sign?'

'Long range vox is still dead, brother. The orks have destroyed all communications infrastructure out here,' said Sunno. 'We are alone. The Emperor is too occupied with greater questions on this world to pay especial attention to us.'

'Salamander Scout reports no sign of xenos activity,' said Ghaskar.

'They are still reporting in?' asked Brusc.

'Yes, with admirable efficiency, my lord,' said Ghaskar. Brusc was growing to like the lieutenant, there was nothing in Ghaskar's tone that suggested he felt he deserved praise for his Salamander crew's diligence.

'It is your decision, brother,' said Sunno.

'You would advise against such a route ordinarily, Brother Sunno,' said Brusc.

Sunno was a veteran of many wars, dangerously jaded in Brusc's opinion, even though he was much younger than the ancient Sword Brother. 'You know the heart of your brother well. But not this time – we are running out of options. How long can we drive around this Emperor-forsaken wasteland without being discovered? It is a short dash and our other choices are poor. The land either side of the valley is too broken for the haulers. We would have to travel three hundred kilometres to the south, directly to the coast, and take our chances there.'

'My men will fight to their last,' said Ghaskar. 'All you must do, my lord, is give the word.'

'It will not come to that,' said Brusc.

Once more, he thought, the decision falls to me. The last time, Osric fell. The thought caused his shoulders to twitch involuntarily.

My laughter will be a long time in returning, he thought. So many of us have died, and yet I remain? Why, O Emperor? What are your plans for me?

'Brother?' prompted Sunno. 'What are your orders?'

Brusc looked ahead. The air had grown hazy again. On the foreshortened horizon, he could make out a bar of caramel hills. A shadow intimated a cleft in the barrier, surely the river valley. He called up overlays from his suit's logic engine that confirmed this.

Sunno was correct. This would be their last moment of peace.

'We go on,' he said.

An hour later, the Salamander failed to make its routine notification call.

'Here they come!' voxed Sunno.

Dozens of light vehicles came leaping over the dunes' ridges. Ork attack buggies, half-tracks, junkers – all equipped with heavy weapons, no two the same. Bikes, ridden by wild-eyed monsters, formed a surging arrowhead around them that constantly threatened to break apart. Four light transports, bursting with xenos, came behind. They were so caked in dust and ash that it was impossible to see which sub-grouping they belonged to. Brusc suspected speed cultists, but ultimately it did not matter.

'Ignore the bikes, and prioritise the transports,' he ordered the others.

The orks were on them quickly, driving at reckless speed.

He snapped off a bolt, catching an ork biker square in the chest. Its ribcage exploded, making it flop like a gutted fish. The bike continued on for a dozen metres, before falling and tumbling over and over in a ball of scattering scrap. Cackling ork outriders skidded around it, bike engines howling. They leaned over in the saddle, firing pistols. The Jopali replied, ruby las-light stabbing out from cabs and containers. The socket stubbers on the cabs rattled. The Chimeras either side of the convoy belted out multi-laser and heavy bolter-rounds, while Doneal covered the front of the convoy with *Cataphraxes*'s storm bolter, and the Taurox covered the rear.

An ork bike went hurtling away from the line of trucks, rearing up as it hit the valley sides. Another exploded. But the riverbed was rough, the orks fast, and many of the Imperial shots went wide.

A line of heavy calibre solid shot stitched holes along the top of Brusc's trailer, punching through the thin sheet metal. The bullets tracked upwards, streaking off Brusc's armour. The Jopali were not so lucky. One was kneeling to get a better aim. He was caught in the shoulder and sent screaming from the rooftop. Another, lying flat, was pierced by bullets coming from below. He jerked twice, his lasgun clattering over the side of the truck. His body slid after it, dangling from his safety rope.

The ork gunner snarled, bashing his driver on the head. He gestured at Brusc. The buggy wobbled as the driver warded off the gunner's blows and glanced up to see what his comrade was so angry about.

'You will make no trophy of me,' said Brusc. He levelled his boltgun. His first shot missed, his aim spoiled by the hauler's sudden jolting. His second went true, decapitating the driver. The headless corpse slumped over the steering wheel, sending it caroming away from the convoy. It slammed into the valley side. The gunner recovered, and traversed his gun for a parting shot. He never made it, falling dead over his own weapon, felled by a sniper rifle.

'A good shot, Marcomar,' said Brusc.

The orks pursued undaunted. More bikes came out of the hills to run alongside the convoy, looping far out so that they could come at the trucks again and again with guns spitting. There were so many now that they were swirling around the giant trucks like flies around cattle. Three buggies and a half-track were harrying the last hauler but one, riddling the sides of the trailer with holes. It drove on, but Brusc doubted there would be anyone left living within. The Taurox Prime rearguard cleared wide areas of the dead river of hostiles, only for them to flood back.

Two of the rickety transports swooped down on a Chimera, chased by a couple of buggies. The tank's turret tracked round, shooting a barrage of fire from its multilaser, and a brave gunner added to the weight of fire with the vehicle's pintle stubber. A fusillade of rockets hammered into the human tank. Poorly fashioned, most clanged off the armour without detonating, but one flew true and exploded against the Chimera's turret. The crewman was obliterated, the turret lifted half off its mount. The buggies closed in on the wounded vehicle.

One buggy went cartwheeling away, its tyres blown out. Another of the transports exploded in an orange fireball, destroyed by shots from the trailing Chimera, but the other drew alongside, easily keeping pace. A dozen orks were crammed into it, hanging from handholds along the outside. A broad gangplank crashed down, hooks on the end catching on the tank's fittings. Ball-mounted lasguns along the side blasted at the xenos, but the gangplank was in the way and they could draw no good lines of fire. With a war cry Brusc could hear over the racket of battle, the orks clambering onto the tank, shoving at each other so hard in their eagerness that one tumbled from the locked vehicles. The Chimera swerved from side to side, trying to shake the orks off, but they only laughed at such entertainment. Within seconds, they had the upper hatch up and were slaughtering every man inside. The linked Chimera and buggy stopped, the orks dancing madly on their prize.

'How much further, Brother Sunno?' asked Brusc.

'Another seventy kilometres until we reach the outermost Imperial line. No guarantee there'll be anything there to greet us, Sword Brother. I'm getting nothing on the vox.'

Brusc blasted an ork from the back of a buggy. The roaring of ork engines was deafening. Black smoke billowed around the trucks.

'My lord!' cried a man of Jopal. He pointed to the south side of the valley.

Seven more trucks laden with orks were coming down the slope, swelling the number of greenskins. Orks swinging grappling irons and the boarding ramps held high on both sides of all the trucks left no doubt in Brusc's mind as to their intentions. In the Rhino's cupola, Doneal swung round and gunned for them with *Cataphraxes*'s storm bolter. His aim was good: the bolts raking across the bed of one of the trucks, slaughtering orks. Brusc added his fire, killing more. Marcomar slew a driver, sending a truck into a swerve that toppled it, spilling orks all over the valley floor. Others were too well protected and his las-shots were halted by iron plating.

'Brother!' warned Marcomar.

A buggy was driving right by the hauler that followed Brusc's. The tractor unit's heavy stubbers could not reduce their elevation enough, their bullets raising tracks in the desert a good metre out from the buggy. Men gesticulated, their shouts inaudible as they leaned out from the container roof. One slipped and fell, hanging helplessly by his ankle cord. Another two stood to help him and were shot down. Brusc switched targets, targeting the buggy. He missed twice, a third round bringing a plume of steam from the buggy's engine block to no noticeable effect.

Its gunner had abandoned his gun. He reached down. When he stood upright he held a large bomb.

A daring jink from the driver brought the buggy between the two haulers. The gunner attached the bomb to the radiator grille of the tractor unit. The driver of the hauler accelerated, trying to crush them, but with a flurry of obscene gestures from the gunner the buggy was away.

'Get down!' Brusc screamed.

To the credit of the driver of the second hauler, he realised his fate and turned sharply, taking the vehicle out of the convoy. A selfless move, but too late.

The bomb exploded, hollowing out the tractor unit. It bounced as it came to a halt, jackknifing into the path of the remaining north flank Chimera. The tank ran into it at speed, clanging to a sudden stop against the flaming wreck. The trailer detached, rolling over the towing bed of the tractor, and reared up. Men flew from it, helpless as ragdolls. It twisted, carried forwards by its own momentum, to land diagonally across the river bed.

The third hauler ploughed into it, sending men skidding off its roof. The stricken vehicles were immediately assaulted. The amount of return fire from them was inadequate. Brusc held his breath, but the other haulers avoided the smash, swerving around the wreckage. A small measure of retribution was earned when one ran over a careless buggy, crushing it under massive wheels. The Taurox gunned down a good number of the orks attacking the survivors as it sped by.

'Do not stop! Drive on! Drive on!' ordered Ghaskar. 'If we stay to aid our comrades, we shall all die!'

'We lost two,' said Brusc to Sunno.

A gleeful howling drew his attention. Two of the fresh ork trucks had survived and were running hard by his trailer. Orks slammed hooked lines into the thin sides of the container, catching the access ladders with others, and swarmed up onto the roof.

They were quick, roaring with battle lust. Two were dropped by lasgun shots and fell back, knocking another ork from his purchase, then the rest were on the roof. The four remaining men of Jopal were dead before Brusc could shout at them to get behind him. Marcomar went on as if nothing were happening, coolly sniping high-value targets away from the truck. Commendable, thought Brusc.

Brusc dropped his boltgun. It clattered on the metal, skittering across the bouncing roof. His chainsword and bolt pistol were in his hands in an instant. He had no time to attach their lanyard chains to his wrists.

'No pity. No remorse. No fear!' bellowed Brusc. In truth, there was no need for such words; he could feel none of these things for the greenskins, they were vermin to be slaughtered. His hatred of them constricted his throat, strangling his battle-hymns. He stood firm, locked to the roof, as the orks attacked.

The first died from a bolt-round to its thick skull. The second fell screaming from the roof, holding its entrails into its belly. Marcomar drew his bolt pistol, shooting down orks trying to crawl up the rear of the truck. To the front, Sunno pulled *Cataphraxes* clear of the convoy, allowing Doneal to target the orks still aboard their trucks next to the hauler. He shredded the rearmost with a concentrated burst of fire, and it came away smashed to nothing by the convoy.

'Die!' screamed Brusc, his spittle coating the inside of his visor. His fury was unbounded. 'You will pay for the death of Brother Osric! You will pay for the lives of every human your miserable kind has taken!'

An ork managed to get a blow past his guard, slamming down a crudely fashioned axe into his pauldron. The force behind it was phenomenal and he swayed back, with only the maglocks of his boots holding him in place. His sensorium buzzed his system with pseudo-pain, informing him that his pauldron was cracked. The ork did not get a chance to strike again. Brusc blew its guts out of its back. It was still snarling as it fell away.

Something landed at his feet. He caught sight of a fizzing stick grenade before it exploded and the roof collapsed beneath his feet.

He landed hard on his back, looking up at a hole in the ceiling of the trailer container. Panicked men were packed into bunks lining the inside. Medicae personnel reached for their sidearms. Brusc got to his feet as a pair of monsters jumped in after him. The first landed on Brusc's chest. He caught its foot and sent it sprawling backwards.

It crashed back into a rack of bunks, the weight of it alone enough to kill the injured men lying there. The second landed behind him. Before the first could rise, it died, its face blown apart. Sister Rosa nodded at Brusc from the far end of the container, a small calibre bolter in her hand.

He had no time to thank her. The second ork was on him, wrenching at his power pack with huge grasping hands. Brusc and the ork staggered backwards. He reached over his head, slapping at the plasteel of his armour before finding the flesh of the ork's hand. He grasped it in a crushing grip, tearing it free of his battleplate. Turning around under the ork's arm, he yanked hard, pulling it off balance and locking its arm. The ork was a mass of knotted muscle, stronger in truth than Brusc, but Brusc was the more skilled warrior. A blow of his forearm bent the thing's elbow the wrong way, shattering it. The ork roared, maw revealing a wealth of yellow fangs. Its uninjured hand went for a big knife at its belt. Brusc smashed the knife from its fingers with his fist, his returning swing throwing the ork's arm wide and exposing its torso. Brusc knocked it down with a kick to its sternum. Such a blow would have pulped the chest cavity of a man, but the ork was not even stunned. Brusc leapt onto it before it could get up again, pinning it to the floor with his knees. He held its good arm down and closed his other hand around its throat.

'Suffer not the unclean to live, suffer not the alien, suffer not the usurper of worlds!' The ork thrashed about, but Brusc would not be dislodged. His armoured fingers dug deeply into its throat. Dark blood ran over them. He wrenched backwards, ripping out its throat. 'O lord Emperor!' he cried, holding up the scrap of flesh. 'Accept this token of blood!'

Incredibly, the ork still lived. Dirty talons scraped at its opened neck, blood bubbled between its teeth, but its eyes gleamed still with hateful life.

'My lord,' called Marcomar from above. 'A brother should guard his wargear with his life.'

Marcomar let Brusc's bolter fall. The Sword Brother stood and caught it in one movement. He levelled it at the ork's head. Unthinking fury glared back.

'I grant you release from your unclean existence.'

The double report of the bolter and the bang of its munition blasting apart the ork's skull killed all sound in the container.

Brusc stared at the thing's ruined face, only vaguely aware of his surroundings.

A massive detonation outside snapped him back to his senses. Brusc's vox crackled into life.

'The orks are retreating, Sword Brother,' said Sunno matter of factly.

'Praise be,' said Brusc, and felt some of the shadow retreat from his heart.

'We should save our thanks, brother,' said Sunno. 'There's a storm coming in.'

ARMAGEDDON HAD NOT quite finished with its convulsions. One last wall of razored ash blasted across the wastes and into the hives. All across the twinned continents of Primus and Secundus the fighting stopped again.

The convoy drove on through the furnace winds laced with cutting ash. The vehicles slowed to a crawl, the remaining haulers rocking on their suspension in the wind.

'Visibility's down to twenty metres,' said Sunno. 'I'm driving blind.'

'Keep on,' ordered Brusc.

'I never said I would not. I trust *Cataphraxes*,' said the dour initiate, his vox roughened by the storm's static.

Brusc sat alone in the damaged trailer. The wounded had been crammed into the other containers as soon as Sunno reported the storm. The Jopali had fixed a tarpaulin over the rent in the room, but it had been torn away as the storm strengthened. Wind whistled through the teeth of the gash. Already ash was building up on the floor, and the air was grey-yellow with suspended particles, coating Brusc's armour.

'Brother,' said Sunno. 'There is an abandoned facility upon my cartographia, very old, but it might give us somewhere to wait this mess out.'

'Head for it,' said Brusc. 'We shall die if we do not.'

A CLEFT IN the rock appeared, wide enough to take the trucks. Brusc stood on loose gravel, eyeing it thoughtfully. After a moment's consideration, he ordered Sunno forward and he walked alongside. Crags materialised out of the haze, tall and wind-worn. He checked the poorly detailed map imagery projected by his helmet. The sole large building and open pit it sat in on the far side of the canyon were unlabelled. 'Is this a mine?'

'Must be,' said Sunno. 'Even if not, we'll be out of the wind. Hidden. No orks are going to be out in this. The humans need their rest.' An edge of derision crept into Sunno's voice.

'That they do,' said Brusc. He did not upbraid Sunno for his tone; it was a sentiment all of the Black Templars expressed. Their crusading spirit, the desire to head ever onward and to destroy the enemies of the Emperor bred into them a certain impatience with weaker men. Brusc was well aware that he felt it; indeed, he had said something similar only days before when they had come to the hospital. Osric had picked him up on it. He always had more patience for the unenhanced, for citizens. Contempt for the weakness of common men was not something Brusc was proud of feeling, but feel it he did. Osric had always been the better man.

He voxed back to Lieutenant Ghaskar, telling him to follow *Cataphraxes* in.

'I will go first,' said Brusc. 'Follow me slowly. Marcomar and Doneal, cover me as best you can.'

Brusc unclipped his bolter. Holding it up to his eyeline ready to fire, he walked into the cleft.

According to his auto-senses, the way through was twelve metres at the nearest widest point. Stone walls rose up either side of him, trammelling the sky into the semblance of an ash-grey river. In the upper reaches of the canyon the wind moaned over the fluted strata of the rock, booming where it encountered cavities. But at the base of the canyon where Brusc walked, the air was unnaturally still. *Cataphraxes*'s engine bubbled behind him, a mechanical chuckle quiet enough that Brusc could still hear the dust falls hissing down from the wastes above. Visibility in the canyon was better than it was in the maelstrom outside, but he still could not see the end. Bulges of rock loomed in the murk, semblances of trees or mythical giants. The red tint of his helmet lenses intensified the effect, making them eerie despite its efforts to delimit the objects it saw for him.

If we are going to be attacked during the storm, it would be somewhere like here, he thought.

He proceeded carefully, gun up, reticule flicking to every dark place in the canyon's wrinkled sides. None proved to be anything more than shadows. The deepest crack was a metre and no more – a simple faulting of ancient stone. The wrong kind of rock for caves, the wrong kind of environment. There was nowhere for anything to hide. Even so, he could not shake the feeling that they were being watched.

He thought he caught a voice and spun round.

'*Brussssscccc*,' he heard. He could swear he heard it, barely louder than the engine and the whine of his armour. '*Brussssccccc*.'

'Anything wrong, brother?' asked Sunno.

Brusc's targeting reticule danced over an ash fall sheeting down, seeking a threat and finding none. His finger relaxed on the trigger of his boltgun.

'No, nothing. The wind. Come on.'

'You are getting nervous, brother,' said Sunno.

'Vigilant,' corrected Brusc. 'Let's pick up our pace. There's nothing here.'

The Sword Brother jogged on. *Cataphraxes*'s engines growled louder as Sunno re-engaged the tracks.

After another hundred metres, the canyon ended.

Brusc took in the wide space before him. Visibility had improved again, the clogged air forming a diffuse ceiling over his head. He could see all the way to the other side of the pit, a disused open-cast mine or quarry. The canyon gave every impression of being naturally formed, but the topography here was anything but. They emerged into a perfect square, the half-kilometre-long edges sharp as if cut out with a knife. On the far side were the dilapidated remains of a facility of some kind. Held off the floor on thick metal pillars, it climbed to the top of the pit wall opposite to a steep roadway that went from floor to edge via several switchbacks. The facility was made of local iron and had reddened in what little moisture there was in the air. He took in the corrosion from both ambient moisture and acid rain squalls and calculated that it had been unused for at least fifty years. More than that, Brusc could tell little about the place. His reticle flicked from point to point, unable to give him any more information than how far away it was, and what windshear would effect his bolts if he were to open fire.

'The mine,' said Sunno.

'Any indication what they were doing here?' asked Brusc. His voice sounded too loud in his helmet.

'It doesn't say,' said Sunno. 'Minimal information. Does it matter, brother?'

'No,' said Brusc. He walked forward until he was standing at the edge of a roadway similar to the one opposite. Evidently, the canyon had been co-opted into being a secondary entrace. The floor of the pit was not uniform. Cuboid sections had been lifted from it. the road headed immediately right from the canyon mouth, a generous arc provided for the turn at the top, three switchbacks taking it to the pit floor. He judged that the trucks would be able to go down, if they were careful. The road continued onwards, skirting the diggings, to the facility. 'I am coming aboard, brother,' said Brusc. 'We will be stopping here tonight.'

NIGHT FELL QUICKLY, hurried in by the ash's gloom. The sky remained thick with ash and glowed strangely with the refracted lights of distant cities, but the pit itself remained clear. Were it not for rare gusts of wind, the mine would have felt like a cave. A stuffy stillness filled the place, the dying gasp of the Season of Fire.

Brusc walked around the camp set up beneath the broken facility. Chutes opened above truck bays ranged against the raw stone of the pit wall. The convoy did not occupy these, but had drawn up in a defensive horseshoe, ends anchored against the pit side. Within this corral there was little activity. Few without orders felt like daring the night; everyone was tired.

Loose sheets of metal banged when the wind gusted. When it did not, the facility groaned as the temperature changed. Bickering voices announced the approach of a Jopali patrol. When they saw Brusc they fell silent. Their sergeant acknowledged him with a nod. Once they thought he was out of earshot they resumed their arguments, their sergeant's threats having little effect.

Brusc watched them go. It was dark under the facility, but his suit picked out their shapes clearly. They reached the inner edge of the camp, and tramped up a set of rickety stairs into the building. Another group was patrolling the road leading out of the pit. He could not see them from his position but they too were arguing and he heard them.

'Keep your men quiet, sergeants,' he growled. 'Unless you want every ork within twenty kilometres to know we're here.'

The Black Templar passed the stairs and headed past the lone sentry guarding the gap between trucks. The man stared at him, afraid of Brusc and the night in equal measure.

He walked along the edge of the trucks, passing more men keeping watch over the pit floor and the road they had entered by. Brusc had the same impression of nervous energy from them all. He walked on until he was clear of the camp and the facility. It towered over him. He should have felt safe beneath it, but somehow he did not.

'The Jopali are staying in their trucks. They don't much like this place.'

'Brother Sunno,' said Brusc as Sunno joined him.

'I have been walking the pit floor.'

'There's nothing down there,' said Brusc.

'It does not hurt to be diligent.'

'You are uneasy?'

Sunno did not reply immediately. 'I'd be a liar if I said I was not.'

Brusc was silent a space. Both of them spoke quietly, but even in the privacy of their helmets their voices felt like an intrusion into the quiet of the pit, as if the animus of the place were offended.

'I have had to break up two fights. It is affecting them. I admit something about it sets my teeth on edge too,' said Brusc.

Sunno looked about himself, his lenses glowing in the flat face of his crusader helm. 'I feel it, I feel it brother. A... A rage.'

'A geologic oddity,' said Brusc. 'Tectonic infrasound, localised magnetic field...'

'Does your armour's spirit detect any of those things? Because mine does not,' interrupted Sunno. 'Perhaps we should not have come here.'

'Perhaps not.' said Brusc. 'Your diligence is correct. Stay so. The storm appears spent. We shall move out at first light.' He looked around. 'You are right, I do not like this place.'

'Yes, Sword Brother,' said Sunno.

Brusc resumed his circuit, skirting around outside the line of giant metal columns supporting the facility. The effect of the sky pressing down was claustrophobic. He experienced a sudden desire to remove his helmet and, seeing no reason not to, he did.

The neck seal hissed as it came undone. The air hit his face like a blast from an oven. Nevertheless, he breathed deeply of it, glad to be able to smell something other than himself and his suit's coolant system. His mutilated face itched terribly, and he rubbed at the patchwork of scars and plasti-skin with armour-clad fingers. Without the red staining of his helm, the mine should have looked less sinister, but his sense of wrongness only grew.

For a moment he closed his eyes. It was so quiet there the silence became almost audible, washing out the distant voices of the Jopali sentries with its roaring hush.

'Brussssccccc.'

Brusc had his bolter in his hands before his helmet hit the floor.

'Who's there?' he shouted. The voice had been louder this time, his name clear. 'Who's there?'

He hunted through the murk. His eyes were keen, but he regretted removing his helmet for he saw nothing. A new set of sounds reached his ears: footsteps scrabbling on loose ash, the thump and jangle of kit bumping on running bodies and the click of respirators.

'My lord, we heard you shouting. Is there something amiss?'

Brusc cursed the men for their clumsiness, no matter how well intentioned. 'Something is out there.' He did not tell them it had spoken his name. 'Gone now.' His delivery made sure they were left in no doubt it had gone because of their racket.

'My lord, I...'

A scream rent the air, confined, bouncing from metal walls.

'The facility,' said Brusc.

The Jopali had no time to respond before Brusc was away running from them. He easily outpaced them, reaching the bottom of the stairs within the camp in seconds. They shook dangerously as he pounded up them, the camp behind him going into a commotion in his wake.

His entrance into the bottom floor of the facility burst the door from its hinges. He squinted into the gloom. The room had been stripped of useful materials, flimsies and yellowed sheets of paper were scattered everywhere, square pale islands on the dark floor. Insubstantial partitions had once divided the place up into administrator's cells. Most were gone, only jagged edges remained where they had been ripped away. A long row of broken windows looked out over the pit. Many had their shutters down. All of these showed signs of storm damage, and several shutters were missing altogether.

The far wall backed onto the rock, the panels that covered it fallen away in places. Only the chutes seemed permanent, giant square pipes pitted by corrosion yet still whole. Everything else was in decay. Acid rain had rotted through large patches of the floor. Through them, past the lumpen silhouettes of broken processing machinery, Brusc saw clear to the roof, an expanse of blackness punctured by holes that, together with the windows, let in the muted glow of the sky. For a moment, he saw the holes as a leering face. Only for a moment. Up there, near the edge of the pit, it was windier. He heard ventilation cowls rotating to face the wind, fans spinning, directing air into spaces that had long since opened themselves to the elements.

That was six floors up. Down at the bottom was only stillness. The room stretched on into an infinity of silences.

A pale figure moved in the gloom.

'Who goes there?' Brusc shouted. The figure stood still for a moment, then walked away out of Brusc's sight, right into the rear wall.

Brusc swore, held his bolter at chest height and advanced.

Army boots clattered on the stairs behind him. The soldiers, seeing Brusc's watchful stance, fanned out with their weapons at the ready. Feeble munitorum torches poked yellow beams of light into the dark.

'Anything to report my lord?' asked Ghaskar.

'Only laxity! I thought you said your men had checked this place?'

'Suflimar!' Ghaskar shouted out of the door. A few seconds later one of his men came up from outside. Ghaskar had a furious exchange with him. Their dialect was so thick that Brusc caught one word in every four.

'He says he did check it, my lord.'

'There's somebody up here. I saw him. About halfway down the hall.'

'Maybe it was Bapoli, or Srinergee. That's who Suflimar left up here, my lord.'

'Where are they now?'

Suflimar called the men's names out, his voice wavering. There was no reply. Vox clicks and mutters asking the sentries to check in produced static hiss.

'Is there another way out of here?' asked Brusc.

'The stairs, down the far end.' Torches converged to pick out a door ajar many metres distant, and broke apart again.

'No. He went out there.' Brusc pointed his gun. 'Halfway down.'

'There is no way out there, my lord,' said Ghaskar.

'The chutes, is there a way into the chutes?' demanded Brusc. 'Or behind the panelling, between the room and the rock?'

'Nay, lord,' Suflimar answered for himself. 'Tere is notting, notting like tat.'

Brusc had thought the lieutenant's faith in his men admirable. Now he saw it as weakness, putting trust in such as these.

'There's one there. You must have missed it,' Brusc snarled. He went forward. The Jopali, unasked, covered him. His armoured feet crunched on broken glass and drifts of ash. The floor was unsteady, and he took care to stick to the joins in the panelling where structural beams ran.

'Brother!' shouted Sunno from outside.

'Enter!' said Brusc over his shoulder.

Sunno jogged up to join his brother. When he reached Brusc he handed him his helmet.

'You dropped this.'

'My thanks, Brother Sunno.'

Sunno's bolter clicked as he brought it up. Brusc maglocked his bolter to his chest while he replaced his helm. Its features revealed to him more clearly by his sensorium, the room looked no less empty. 'Where are the neophytes?'

'Watching over the camp, and keeping Sister Rosa in her trailer. She wanted to come up here.'

'We will not allow it. Something is gravely amiss here. I saw someone. Ghaskar's men are missing.'

'Understood, brother.'

The pair of them spread out, then took oblique lines across the floor toward where Brusc had seen the pale man. In the dark, Sunno's white shoulder pads were a muddy grey, the black templar cross stark upon them. Brusc's own red Sword Brother's cross was invisible on black. He was a shadow giant, armour whining eerily along with the wind above. The weakened floor shifted alarmingly under their great weight, but they did not take their eyes or their guns from their target.

'Brother,' said Sunno. He held his bolter up one handed, pointing with the other. Behind a pile of debris was a body. Brusc's auto-senses showed him what it was before he'd registered it. Data flicked before his eyes. A threat indicator unfolded in the lower left of his vision, and ticked steadily upwards.

'Dead,' said Sunno.

Brusc crunched over to it as stealthily as he could. Close inspection revealed a catalogue of horrors.

'Not just dead. Mutilated.'

The man's jaw had been pulled off, his tongue nearly cut around so that it remained rooted in his head and poked into the air. His eyelids were gone, giving him a crazed stare, as were the tips of his fingers. His stomach had been neatly excised, the guts and the tissue that covered them were neatly piled next to him.

'Temperature reading suggests death occurred recently. Who is this?' Brusc asked. The Guardsmen approached fearfully. One of them clawed off his respirator to be noisily sick.

'Tat Bapoli, lord,' said Suflimar. 'Ork do it?'

'One of their torturers maybe. One of their infiltrators, but I see no trace of their presence. Even the most cunning ork gives himself away.' He searched for dung or disturbances in the rubbish strewing the place, and found none.

'That's not the work of an ork, brother,' said Sunno privately.

'No,' replied Brusc. 'It is not. Speak carefully.'

'Yes, brother.'

'Emperor preserve us,' said Ghaskar.

'We shall all pray that he does,' said Brusc publically. 'Be on your guard! The Emperor will not help those who do not help themselves.'

Sunno advanced further. 'Here's our door.'

With the barrel of his bolter he pointed to a rectangle of blackness in the stone so deep their armour senses could not penetrate it. Suflimar babbled a long stream of his nonsense Low Gothic at the sight of it. The other Jopali became agitated, jabbering back.

'He says that this door was not here three hours ago when he checked, my lord, nor when the last patrol came by,' said Ghaskar.

'And now there is a door, and it is open,' said Sunno. Unlike every other edge in the pit, square cut by mining machinery, this had a rough look, as if hewn by primitive tools. 'It looks like it has been here for a thousand years, brother.'

A whisper came out of the darkness. *'Brusssscccc.'*

Brusc's bolter clicked against his armour as he pulled it in tightly to himself to steady his aim.

'What?' asked Sunno.

'You didn't hear that?'

'Hear what?'

'A whisper,' said Brusc. Realising that their conversation was spooking the men, he switched to vox.

'I heard nothing,' said Sunno.

A scream sounded from the door. Up and up it rose, reaching a crescendo of terror, then collapsed into despairing laughter.

'Now that I heard,' said Sunno. He shifted, seeking a target in the dark.

'Something fell is at work here,' said Brusc. He switched back to helmet speaker. His words were harsh, the voice of the Emperor's deadly angels, and it reassured the men. 'Remain here with my brother. I will enter the dark and see if I can find your comrade. If I do not return within an hour, break camp and depart immediately. Is that understood?'

'Yes, my lord,' said Ghaskar. The men quietened, grateful to have orders.

'Do not waste yourself for one man, brother,' said Sunno.

'There is more at stake than a life,' said Brusc.

'Then let me come with you, brother. Let me help you,' said Sunno.

Brusc was already walking towards the door. Whispering came at him, seemingly from within his helmet.

'If I am right about what I think might be down there, brother,' said Brusc. 'Then only the Emperor can help me.'

He stepped into the door with a prayer on his lips, disappearing from view instantly, his black armour swallowed by the dark.

'What did you hear?' voxed Sunno. 'What did you hear, brother?'

Only static answered.

* * *

THE DARKNESS WAS fleeting. Firelight took its place. Brusc walked down stairs unsuited to human feet. Torches flickered in sconces, too few for the illumination provided. The stairs wound in a spiral, down and down.

'The lord Emperor is my protector. He is the shield of humanity,' said Brusc. 'I am His sword.'

Brusc was old, very old. Six hundred years he had fought for the Imperium, his blooding taking place in the Kalidar Crusade, yet another war against the orks. The following years saw the Black Templars criss-crossing space bled dry to supply Lord Solar Macharius's glorious adventure, and he had fought all manner of foes before he was made an initiate.

But not daemons. He encountered them much later. The Adeptus Astartes were better informed about the nature of the warp, but even amongst them few knew the whole truth. As a Sword Brother of Dorn's black knights, Brusc was one who did.

He had fought daemons. He had killed them. He had seen them suck his brothers' souls from their bodies. He had seen the horror the daemons brought, how they twisted reality about them.

There was a daemon here. The hatred burning unasked for in his twin hearts made him sure of that. His teeth itched, a metallic taste was in his mouth. A sure sign of sorcery. That was the only word fit for it.

'Let the Emperor's light show me the way. Let his light cast perfect brilliance, dividing that which is true from that which is not true. Let it show lies for lies, deceit for deceit.'

His prayer grew louder, until it rang from the walls of the tunnel. In response, his vision shifted, the tunnel becoming the pulsating gut of a great creature. A brief vision that mocked his pleas for veracity, but this falsehood was driven aside by his will.

'Let his light blind my unholy foe. Let his light show me my enemy. I am a son of Rogal Dorn. I am the chosen of the Emperor. I am a vessel for his wisdom and his vengeance. I am a Space Marine of the Black Templars, an adept of the stars, and I know no fear. Show me yourself, I command it.'

A deep, throaty laugh answered, an entirely inhuman sound blended with the purring of predators and the gurgle of sucking wounds. This was a laughter that brought madness.

'Little soldier, little soldier. How you amuse! What power is yours to command me?'

A rasping noise followed, as of scales on stone. A hideous shriek directly blasted Brusc's ears, bypassing the aural dampers of his battleplate. He stumbled, ears ringing, which brought forth another burst of laughter from his unseen opponent that ended in a menacing, polyphonic growl.

Brusc staggered around the final turn of the stairs and came into a stone chamber bathed in blood-red light. An obelisk stood at its centre, made of dark crystal. Multifaceted and irregular in shape, it was pointed at the top and thinned near the base to the width of Brusc's thigh. A domed ceiling, covered in flaking paintings of things out of nightmares, curved over it.

The daemon watched. Long snake coils looped around the obelisk, black scales glinting. The thing was entirely serpentine but for the head. In place of a serpent's face it bore the features of three men. The leftmost and centre were shrunken, dead things, wizened as mummies, but the one on the right regarded Brusc with a vile amusement. A strange smell came from it, not the acerbic stink of reptiles, but an unexpected muskiness, pleasant until deeper breaths revealed undertones of rotting meat.

The chamber resounded with an unsettling babble, many voices, many languages. This uncanny chatter was inconstant in volume, falling below hearing and rising up again until the words were almost clear. The voices were in pain, or they mocked Brusc and his Emperor, or they begged him for an end to suffering or cajoled him to join them. Animal growls and hisses competed with the human sounds. Alien voices were there too. There was nothing of purity in any of it.

The daemon reared up high so that it might look down upon Brusc. This display of superiority from something so low spurred the Black Templar's recovery. Hatred spiked in him, and he pulled himself tall.

'The power of the Emperor is mine. It is the birthright of all men, should they have the strength to call upon it. I am of the Emperor's elect. I am one of his chosen.'

'You are no pysker-soul,' said the daemon.

'Through my faith alone is the Emperor's attention upon me, and He stands by my right hand. Through me, He will slay you.'

'The Emperor. You worship? He is your god?' hissed the daemon. The cacophony of the damned swelled as it spoke and the daemon gurgled a laugh. *'Well. This is novelty not seen for long ages. Only once have I witnessed the cripple of Terra's clone children bleating praises. Their devotion did not end well for them.'*

'No others of the Adeptus Astartes see the truth of the Emperor's light, nor ever have. We alone are the chosen.'

'Do not be so sure, little soldier. There were others, until they saw the truth behind your master's lies. But He is persistent. We grant Him that. Worshipped He is, and worshipped He has been. Foolishness is eternal.'

'The truth saves.'

'Ah! It does, it does! That you are right!' the daemonic serpent swayed sinuously across the room, its body lengthening obscenely. *'Not your truth, for that is a lie. Behold! Here is one who was saved by the truth.'*

The daemon moved aside, revealing a man kneeling beside the obelisk who had not been there before; the second of Ghaskar's sentries. He was facing away from Brusc. At some prompting he turned slowly, revealing his skinless face. He clacked exposed teeth together and said something unintelligible for his lack of lips. Slowly, he raised his hand, and showed the tattered rag of his face. It writhed of its own accord, an expression of utter horror upon it.

'If you wish to worship, this is the way it is done, little soldier. Sacrifice and receive. A simple transaction, more honest than the lies of the Golden King.' The triple head darted forward. A smile played across the thing's plump lips. The dry smell of old decay came from its dead faces. *'Put down your feeble weapon. You cannot harm me. Embrace my masters and know power unbound!'*

Previously unseen runes on the obelisk flared hotly. Brusc took a step back, feeling the heat even through his armour. The disfigured Guardsman held up his arm and burst into flame. He stood unhurriedly, and danced to a toneless song sung by the mocking voices until his entire body blazed. Abruptly, he fell. Even as the fire consumed him in a riot of unnatural pinks and blues, he twitched, jerking along to the daemon-song until he could move no more. Brusc shut off his air intakes, the smell of burning flesh and the daemon's stink too much. It had no effect, and the smell somehow infiltrated the machinery of his battleplate, growing stronger, making his head swim. His altered body worked harder to clear his system of toxins to no avail. The daemon leaned in very close, putting its face close to his helmet visor. Brusc found he could not move. The smell of perfume and spoiled blood was overpowering.

'Battle you have fought.' A long black tongue, suckered like the arm of a squid, ran up the crack of his pauldron. *'War comes ever to this world. I came for one such war, with the Primarch Angron and his daemon-legions. He has gone, but I remain.'*

'Liar,' said Brusc through numb lips. He was salivating furiously, drool spilled down his chin.

'And who was the First War fought against, oh most noble son of the corpse lord? It is a secret closely kept. Do you know? No rebellion was the first war, but glorious invasion.' The head darted to one side, then the other, the daemon's face twisted with wicked delight as it appraised him. *'And all the wars before that.'*

Brusc raged inside at his easy subdual, powerless against the daemon's sorcery.

'I know you, Brusc, I know much. Honour and glory, glory and honour, these things are everything to you. To fight and to die in noble cause. Six centuries you have scurried from one end of the galaxy to the other on the errands of your false god. What a waste of your potential, such a squandering of devotion.' The words hissed from the daemon's mouth, becoming ever more snakelike.

Images of Brusc's life forced themselves into his mind. His elevation, his blooding, his time with Brother Adelard... Years and years of war and service, years of suffering.

'So long it took for your accession to the Sword Brethren. They did not repay you easily for your efforts. So long to wait, and the victory so hollow when it came.'

Brusc could no longer speak. He remembered the honour duels. Three times he had tried his hand in the Circle of Honour. Only on the third did he succeed. Five hundred years old then. So long to wait. He railed against the daemon's words and was horrified to realise they were, in part, true. He had been overlooked. He had been neglected. Why, surely he was worthy of a Marshal's badge?

'All that faith and fire. And for what?' the daemon said, its voice become seductive.

A torrent of memories were unlocked in Brusc's mind, all of them of Osric. Osric, his last neophyte. Osric, the finest friend he had had in all his long years. Osric as a boy, as neophyte, as an initiate.

Osric dead, slain by the orks only days before. Osric brought low by the same desire for hollow honour.

Brusc howled, a formless bellow of grief and anger. There had been no time to allow himself the luxury of mourning. There never was enough time.

'Yes, you see, little soldier. The Emperor takes and takes and takes. What does He give you? Nothing. In a moment I will make you an offer. He has already stripped you of your precious humanity. What use to you is a soul?'

Brusc saw it in his mind's eye, the daemon leaning in intimately, its breath tickling his cheek somehow through the plasteel of his helmet.

'This is what you will receive from your new gods.'

Brusc walking through fire, his armour changed. Fanged maws decorating his backpack's vents, spikes on his shoulders. His head bare and tattooed, his broken face a study in delight as he gunned down dozens of Imperial soldiers. Other battles crowded his thoughts, many triumphs.

'In your might you will bestride worlds. In your honour you will be unmatched.'

Great honour was bestowed upon him by raucous gatherings of others like him, renegades and the dispossessed. Men and demigods flocked to his banner. Above all was pleasure, pleasure at his power, to do as he would. This was his true potential.

'There is no pleasure in your life. I can give you much. Others have come to me. Others have accepted. Others have prospered.' Visions now of these men and women. Some drawn here in war, others in peace, all hungering for something more. Mutant, human, and post-human too. **'They had their greatest desires fulfilled. And who can blame them? What does your corpse lord offer, but the ignominy of slow defeat, hellish suffering as your worlds burn, holding back the fires of the truth. Here is my offer.'**

The serpent leaned in as it had in the vision. As it had in the vision it spoke, words that Brusc could never remember, and yet which haunted him nightly for the rest of his days.

The Emperor protects! The Emperor protects! thought Brusc. *Release me that I might do my duty.*

'What is your response?'

A million memories pounded through his mind, a new humiliation with every heartbeat. He had achieved nothing. He was nothing, but he could be something.

Brusc was tempted, oh, he was tempted. He would spend many days and nights in contemplation, watched over by his Chaplains.

But he did not succumb.

'No,' said Brusc.

His defiance freed him. Brusc's limbs were his own to command. He raised his bolter. His armour thrummed in anticipation.

'Fool, you cannot harm me,' said the daemon. Its eyes glowed dangerously. *'No mortal weapon can pierce my skin. You will die, and I will remain. I always remain.'*

Brusc opened fire, not upon the daemon, but upon the obelisk.

The creature had told the truth regarding its flesh. Where Brusc's bolt-rounds hit they detonated harmlessly on the scales. But the majority of his shots smashed into the stone, knocking chips free as they exploded.

'Stop!' hissed the snake, and the sunken eyes of its mummified face opened and their mouths began to scream. It dived at him, spitting pinkish venom that smoked upon his armour. Brusc rolled under its head, bolter always firing, concentrating his rounds upon the weaker section of the obelisk towards the base. Sparks flew from it. With each shot, the daemon keened louder, and the voices in the air wailed.

His gun ran empty, and Brusc ran at the obelisk. Again its inner fire blazed. His battleplate trilled alarms at him, his coolant system struggling to prevent him being cooked alive.

Brusc dodged the daemon's weaving body, and aimed a kick at the upper part of the stone. He hit it with both feet and fell onto his back. The weakened neck of the obelisk splintered. It turned on the fracturing stump, and fell sideways.

'Fool! Fool! Free! I am freeeeeeeee!' howled the daemon.

There was a burst of light and a hateful snarl, and then all was dark.

Time passed. It could have been an age. Brusc was disoriented, his armour inactive. It took him some time to realise he had been buried alive.

His limbs were immovable. He was trapped.

A lesser man in such straits would have panicked, or fought his fate. Brusc did not. Even with his armour barely functioning he would not die for some time. After trying to mentally impel it to awaken, he gave up and lay there in silent prayer, thinking on what he had seen, trying to deny that he had been tempted. He could not.

Scraping reverberated in his helm. Something grabbed his arm. An armoured hand. Then there were more hands grasping him, slipped under his limbs, pulling at him. His plate rang with the blows of entrenching tools digging.

'Brother, brother!' said Sunno urgently. 'Do you live?'

Brusc spoke weakly; without amplification his voice was muffled.

'Yes. I am alive.'

'Praise be!' shouted Sunno joyously, and was joined by the neophytes. The faces of Jopali Indentured crowded round him.

Readouts flickered in Brusc's helmplate. A building whine saw his power plant restart, and strength returned to his battleplate's limbs. He pushed himself up, ash and sand running off his armour in rivulets, and was hauled by eager hands from the hole he had been in. He expected to be deep in the rock, and so it took him a moment to place himself. He was not underground, not in the facility, not even close – the roofs of the building he could see half a kilometre away. He was instead in a square excavation pit in the greater body of the mine delvings. He was outside, exactly opposite to the direction he had gone.

'What happened?' said Sunno, taking in the acid-pitting of his armour. He reached out to touch the damage. Brusc caught his wrist.

'Another time brother. There are too many watching.' He nodded at the Guardsmen around them.

'Did you find Srinergee?' asked Ghaskar.

'I am sorry to report that he is dead, lieutenant.'

'How?'

Brusc ignored the question. He examined the delving. He could not be sure, but there was an irregularity to the sides at the bottom that spoke to him of a broken stone dome, and that if they dug downwards they would find the toppled obelisk and the remains of Srinergee.

The day was clear for Armageddon, with yellow skies and a weak sun. The only ash remaining was high in the stratosphere. The rest had fallen, or been blown further on. He listened intently, searching for that seductive voice, but all he heard were the sounds of the men shifting uneasily around him, all eyes on him. Noises came from the camp. Shouts, the sounds of engines being tested, made weak by distance – sounds comforting in their prosaic nature.

His sense of unease, however, had not deserted him. A gust of wind stirred the sand. The last of the day. The last, he always remembered it, of the Season of Fire. Carried upon this breeze, he thought he heard a chilling laugh.

'We must leave this place,' he said. 'We must leave immediately, and we must never return.'

ABOUT THE AUTHOR

Guy Haley is the author of the Space Marine Battles novel *Death of Integrity*, the Warhammer 40,000 novels *Valedor* and *Baneblade*, The Beast Arises novel *Throneworld*, and the novellas *The Eternal Crusader*, *The Last Days of Ector* and *Broken Sword*, for *Damocles*. His enthusiasm for all things greenskin has also led him to pen the eponymous Warhammer novel *Skarsnik*, as well as the End Times novel *The Rise of the Horned Rat*. He has also written stories set in the Age of Sigmar, included in *War Storm*, *Ghal Maraz* and *Call of Archaon*. He lives in Yorkshire with his wife and son.

CALGAR'S SIEGE

PAUL KEARNEY

An extract from
CALGAR'S SIEGE
by Paul Kearney

'Fidelis, this is *Alexiad*,' Calgar said. 'Do you read?'

The vox came back with a series of explosions stunning it. Calgar winced at the shrill squawk of them.

A sizzling, intermittent comm. 'We read you.' It was not Tyson.

'Break off, repeat, break off and make an emergency warp jump. You cannot stay here. Jump and make for Seventh Company if you can. Do you acknowledge?'

No answer.

'*Fidelis* is burning,' Markos said in a low voice.

There was a crash in the stern and the Thunderhawk was shunted forward as though given an enormous slamming kick from behind.

'Fighter-bombers on our tail,' the dorsal gunner said. 'I count eight, no, nine–'

Then an immense explosion struck the *Alexiad*. Calgar was thrown forward in his restraints, then back again.

One of the Ultramarines further down the hold was knocked partially free of his harness. Proxis grabbed the battle-brother's arm in his own massive gauntlet and held him fast.

'Losing atmosphere in the hold,' Calgar said calmly, studying the readout in his bionic eye. 'Helm up, prepare for vacuum.' He locked down his own helm with its corvid beak, and it immediately took over the relay feed. He could see more clearly now. The compartment was filling with smoke.

'Emergency landing, brother,' he said to Markos. 'Put her down anywhere you can.'

'Main engines offline,' Markos came back. 'We're working with retros only. Dorsal gun gone. My lord, I have failed you.'

'We will discuss that later,' Calgar said. The atmosphere hit them like a wall, and the battered Thunderhawk bucked and leapt under them. There was a series of tearing crashes, and Calgar watched the readout and noted with approval that both Markos and Dextus were launching every missile they had, lightening the two gunships and ridding them of dangerous ordnance. The ramshackle ork fighter-bombers were trying to stay close, but even as he watched the feed, he saw three of them wink out, no doubt battered apart by the rough orbital entry.

'Stand by for crash landing,' Markos said over the *Alexiad*'s vox.

Calgar watched the shimmering data feed inside his helm, the altitude warnings roaring a red klaxon inside the compartment. The ork fighters were peeling off, what was left of them. They were trying to regain orbit, their systems being shredded by the thick atmosphere of Zalidar.

And it was the *Fidelis* they were after, most of all. A single pair of Thunderhawks was poor pickings.

They don't know I am on board, Calgar realised. Well, thank the Throne for that at least.

The readout went dark. Calgar blinked, but it was dead – the onboard cogitator systems had failed. He was as blind as the rest of those inside the hold, a mere passenger being rattled around a punctured, broken tin can that was hurtling to earth almost uncontrolled.

His enhanced hearing still caught the shriek of the airbrakes, and the grating roar of the forward retros. Markos was trying to bring her nose up. His suit systems noted a change in the outside atmosphere and automatically shifted from vacuum mode to save power. The air in his helm tasted different, and was warmer. He was breathing the air of Zalidar for the first time.

'Brace for impact,' Markos said over the Chapter vox, and Calgar repeated the phrase out loud for the sake of the storm troopers in the bow, raising the volume with his suit speakers. Even so, he was not sure they would have heard over the roar and rattle of their headlong descent.

Gravity and G-forces were clamping him down – he could feel them even through the artificer power armour he wore.

A crash forward, not an explosion, more as if they had hit something yielding. The nose was up – Markos was working wonders with the crippled ship – and then another thunderous bang. Thank the Emperor's mercy that the prow of the Thunderhawk was heavily armoured.

Then there was a sensation as though an immense hammer had slammed into them. Calgar had a glimpse of broad daylight as a chunk was torn out of the bow. The ship cartwheeled and whirled in a dizzying series of leaps and crashes, the massive craft tumbling like a stone tossed downhill. He glimpsed vegetation, green, then blue sky, then the limbs of trees torn off and sent flying through the compartment.

A final, withering crash, and then all was black and silent.

Order the novel or download the eBook
from *blacklibrary.com*
Also available from